Acknowledgements

I just want to thank the hundreds, if not thousands of solid dudes that I was incarcerated with at both Jesup, GA & Bennetsville, SC FCI. Thanks for reading and critiquing this book. You guys were my biggest supporters and because of that I developed confidence and was able to take my passion and talent to the next level. And to my mother, sisters, brothers, cousins, and homies that never forgot about me during my 12 year bid, word's can't explain my gratitude. Our time is now. I do this for yall the most.

Special thanks to my hittas on 31 & Jefferson. Rip my uncle Rico, Willy D, Bullet, Tony, lil D, and so many others. You all are living through me. My stories are a direct reflection of the life we once lived.

A Message From The Author

I wrote this to shine the light on the corruption that's often found within the judicial system. Though laws were created to regulate the behavior of the civilian population, often times, they're financially driven and contradicting. So I bring awareness to this through my characters Press and Agent Love.

I experienced police brutality first hand. Back in 2005 I was lied on in a courtroom by a group of conniving narcotics agents (CNT). The same CNT agents that arrested me were fired for corruption. But the damage had already been done. I spent a significant portion of my life behind bars as a result. With that said, I WILL NOT shut up about this topic. What should've killed me only made me stronger. After being incarserated for twelve years, I'm here to redeem the truth and finally set the record straight.

But the problem is bigger than police brutality. Although the media would have you thinking otherwise, especially in light of this new phenomenon of cops killing unarmed teens. Black lives do matter. But all cops are not bad. So to all the law enforcement, military personel, and good cops out there, yall should stand with us, not against us. United we stand, *divided* we fall. The government don't give a shit about yall neither.

The bigger problem is our government, on both a local and federal level. We, as in the masses, need to regain control. The United States of America was founded on democracy. That means that we, the people, represent the real separation of powers, judicial, executive, and legislative.

Copyrights

Disclaimer

This is a work of fiction. Names, characters, business's, places, events, locales, and incidents are either the products of the author's imagination or used in a fictitious manner. Any resemblance to actual persons, living or dead, or actual events is purely coincidental.

CHAPTER I

In the beginning

Silence surrounded the atmosphere. The only available sound besides that came from the trunk of a sabotaged convertible. The music was blasting loud in the inside, but the muffler, the piece located on the front of the car, was louder. No sound was found, within a two-mile radius, other than the vehicle reference above.

Normally, the environment would be filled with chaos, marijuana-smoke, and sirens. However, on this particular night, it was surprisingly peaceful. For now. Homicide would soon be a major part of tonight's events. Tonight, in Savannah Georgia, the seed would be planted that later sparked the revolution.

After pulling up to a local gas station, officer Mcgurt unfastened his seatbelt. He was in a rush to refill his gas tank with petro. Spotting a crackhead pacing the parking lot with a bucket of water, he lowered his music. He wasn't in the mood to tolerate any begging attempts. He just wanted to take his money, pump his gas, and leave, just like everyone else did, without the hassle.

Annoyed, Officer Mcgurt opened the driver's door with an attitude.

"No Thanks," Officer Mcgurt blurted, slamming the door shut before the smoker could even open his mouth. The crackhead had on an oversized sweatshirt, run down pair of Nikes, and a pair of old navy jeans, all of which was the sole reason the smoker approached the car. He was trying to sell the very clothes that he had on.

Officer Mcgurt's seven-year-old son, little press, sat quitely in the passenger seat trying to make some sense out of his observations.

"Dad?"

"Yes son."

"Why does he want to sell his clothes?"

"Good question. Why don't you ask him?"

"I would. But he smells bad."

"So I take it you don't wanna shake his hand?"

Little press shook his head.

Officer Mcgurt laughed in response.

"Smart kid. Son. Imma run in here to get gas. You pump. And try not to waste it like you did the last time. Deal?" officer Mcgurt joked, as he hopped out of his vehicle cautiously. Officer Mcgurt was in the process of entering the store. But his attempt was futile. After a series of pleas, little press convinced his dad to let him go pay for the gas instead. Entering the store now, little press smiled harder than a SNAP recipient with a EBT deposit. Anxious, he grabbed three sodas out of the deep freeze while he gathered his premature thoughts.

I just dodged a bullet. That was a close call. One Pepsi for me, one for mommy. None for dad. He's too stingy. Besides, he doesn't wanna buy me no' m & m's and skittles. Now, I can steal.

Smoke stood angrily in the aisle of the "parkers" store preplanning his attack. He analyzed the surveillance cameras and positioned himself out of their sight as he fumbled with his thoughts.

Is my fitted cap hiding my face enough? How long will this shit take? Behave ol man. Don't wanna have to kill you.

Spotting some kid coming down the aisle, Smoke snapped back into reality. The kid wore a pair of adidas but he had a set of ears that would put Will Smith to shame. Dumbo had to be little man's name Smoke thought. He watched as the kid stuffed varies pieces of candy inside of his pants. Smoke wasn't surprised by the kid's display of ignorance. It was painfully obvious that the boy was an amateur thief.

In the midst of seeing the kid get his 5-finger discount on, Smoke saw an angy Chinese man approach which caught him completely off of guard. Placing his hands inside of his hoody, smoke gripped his gun, wrapping his index finger around the hair pin trigger instinctively. He was prepared for a showdown.

Surprisingly, the man walked right pass Smoke in an urgent manner. This was very confusing. Until he realized that the old Chinese man was at a disadvantage.

Following this event, Smoke slid an old revolver from the compartment of his hoody. His wicked thoughts were going into overdrive.

Dumb ass ol' man. He's slippin. This shit is gonna be easier than I thought. Like taking candy from a baby.

All little press could think about was his pockets, which was filled with lynth, and sugary content. He couldn't wait to get home to eat it all. This was a "smooth getaway" he said proudly to himself. This was his best performance todate. He played the role to the t, and as a result, he was two packs of m & m's and skittles richer. He was the man. Or boy.

Looking to his right, little press saw a suspicious looking black guy draped in black. The man had on a black hoody, hat, and pants, all of which complimented his charm oil like skin. The suspicious guy was trying to cover his eyes but he was doing a poor job.

Feeling his shirt being snatched, little press dropped his sodas not sure what happened.

"You, you, you. You steal, no pay, the angry Chinese man said using a hint of broken english. You try steal no pay. I call police on child thief. Three time steal no pay, I call police!" The man threatened, dragging little press along.

Little press prayed for a miracle as he thought about his near future. This is why his dad didn't want him in the store alone in the first place because he had already been caught stealing previously. Now this. And jail. He couldn't do any time he thought scarily, he was only seven. The jail bullies would eat him alive the moment he arrived. And whenever he did get out (if that was even possible) his dad would beat the black off of his behind. Hell, his butt cheeks had just resumed to its normal color and the last incident happened months ago.

And then it happened. His prayers were answered. God had not abandoned him after all. He watched as Smoke hit the Chinese man upside the head with the gun twice.

BAP! BAP!

Realizing how blessed he was, little press thanked God silently, secretly praying that Smoke's heart was as black as he was.

◆ ◆ ◆

After the Chinese man fell to the floor, Smoke stomped him twice in the face."Now get yo old ass up and take me to DA'MONEY!" Smoke roared, causing blood to explode from the man's head.

After searching every aisle, Smoke made everybody in the

store come to the front and lay down on the floor face down. A second assailant, who just appeared out of nowhere, locked the door in the process.

Smoke made the Chinese man take him to the back office where a small safe was located. After prying the safe open, the man handed Smoke a bag.

"Three grand? What the fuck's this? U wanna die mufucka? I know u got more than dat!"

"No lie, no lie, please take", the old man cried creating a diversion. He then reached for his own gun swiftly.

Smoke never saw it coming. Two shots fired, grazing him across the stomach. After a series of fighting over control of the man's gun, Smoke finally managed to overpower him and confiscate his firearm. Then Smoke shot'em. Twice, one time in the chest, and another in the head. Instantly, the old man's body dropped like a bad habit. The heavy impact was so loud that it sounded like a marching band.

Nervous, Smoke made sure that he had all the money before exiting the office. Upon his return to the front of the store he noticed that the police was outside. He could see the flashing lights from inside.

Who called them? I'll never surrender. I Just need some insurance.

Thinking this, Smoke made his way over to the floor, next to the innocent bystanders. He made a rapid choice and snatched one of the older ladies.

"*Pleeeease. Nooooo,*" the old lady cried, as Smoke placed the gun to the tip of her forehead, forcing her along.

"Bitch, what the fuck you looking at? He yelled to one of the onlookers as his hat fell off.

"You aint never seen a nigga with a ugly haircut before, TURN YO BALD'HEAD'ASS AROUND!"

Nobody would come between Smoke and his three-grand. Even

if it meant having a shootout with the police. These were his thoughts as he stepped out the store holding the elderly lady as a hostage.

◆ ◆ ◆

Twelve-year old Tanaka sat in the back office crying his poor little heart out. Hysterical, he couldn't believe what had just happened, it was just too brutal. His dad was laying on the floor, DEAD. The smell of his rotten corpse polluted the air causing Tanaka to become lightheaded not only from the sent but from the experience. The fact that his dad was deceased was hard to digest. He was an American citizen but his dad moved to the united states from China prior to his birth. His mom was a two-dollar hooker that sold her body to the wicked streets of Savannah and he hardly ever saw her.

Tanaka was instructed to call the police on the black kid, little press, the minute his dad rolled back the survelliance footage. Needless to say the proper authories would soon arrive, because this theft, no matter how small, was captured on video.

Looking at the corpse, Tanaka fell on the floor into a fetal position, pouring out all of his emotions uncontrollably. Now, he was all alone.

CHAPTER 2
Comas and bullets

Exactly forty eight hours later, Officer Mcgurt was miraculously awaken from an induced coma. Sweating like OJ Simpson on trial back in 1994, Officer Mcgurt in took his surrounding. The hospital bed. The gown. The white sheets. Everything   was unclear to him at this point and for some reason he just couldn't remember how he ended up inside of a hospital bed.

"Nice to have you back with us Officer Mcgurt," Doctor Zuckerburg, a professor of anesthesiology and neurological surgery, greeted, welcoming him back into reality. For the past two days officer mgcurt had been desperately fighting for his life. But things were looking better for him now because he was slowly regaining his consciencessness.

"You were placed in a Medically Induced Comma, also known as a MIC. This happens often in cases with traumatic brain injuries—such as the one you experienced. Since you were shot in the head the purpose is to ensure the control and protection of the brain dynamics," informed the Anesthesiologist.

"Your very lucky to be alive."

Shortly after, Doctor Zuckerburg left the couple to themselves. Conscience, Officer Mcgurt remained silence. He was thinking.

Shot in the head? Me?

"Baby. Are you awake? Thank you", Clarissa mouthed, acknowledging the big man upstairs. Looking to his left, officer Mcgurt noticed his wife sitting in the dark alone. She just sat there, weeping, on and off, for 48 hours.

Officer Mcgurt tried to speak but his attempts were halted. Clarissa placed her perfectly manicured finger tips on his lips. "Doctor Zuckerburg wants you to get your rest. So please. Don't speak—*Relax.*"

"Baby? Can you still hear me? The doctor also said that the bullets penetrated through your chest, several of them. He said dat, dddat...Clarissa stuttered dramatically, eyes moistening by the minute. He said dat you'd be paralyzed if the bullets would've traveled inside of you any further."

"They had to remove your right lung during surgery. But you probably couldn't feel it because they gave you some extremly powerful anesthesia. So sad baby. You were in a coma for two days."

Two days? How?

"Where's our son?" Officer Mcgurt finally found the strength to utter.

"With mama. I think it's better if he doesn't see you like this, Clarissa explained. Ten minutes of silence passed before the conversation continued. Preston. We need you. Your son needs you. I need you. And what would've happened if we lost you? Hun? Mister big bad cop. What was I gonna tell our son? That his dad died during the call of duty? Died for the Justice System? That doesn't give a shit about him?" Clarissa cried, emotions being replaced by anger.

"Your job is not worth your life. The academy isn't helping us out with the mortgage. We can't even cover these hospital expenses," Clarissa continued to complain as she placed her head into her lap. Clarrissa, officer mgcurt's spouse, was oblivious, and depressed.

Officer Mcgurt held his breath as he struggled with his thoughts.

Now here I am, in a hospital bed, Missing a right lung, and explan-

ation, and all she could think about is the mortgage. Women

Not in the mood to argue, officer Mcgurt pretended to fall back asleep as he tapped his memory banks for directions to memory lane.

Officer Mcgurt remembered stopping by the Parkers gas station. Somehow, his son, little press, convinced him to let him pay for the gas instead. After ten minutes passed, he remembered becoming agitated because the gas pump failed to click on which suggested that his son hadn't paid for the petro.

See, that's why I didn't want him in there in the first place. Silly, that boy of mine. Can't wait until he come out. He don't know when to quit.

Curious, Officer Mcgurt went to investigate, only to discover that the place was being robbed. He went ballistic.

Mad because he left his cell phone at the house, Officer Mcgurt ran back to his car. By the time he returned a random stranger was there. The guy had just walked up and noticed the robbery himself. He also noticed that mcgurt had a nine-millimeter glock.

"Wow. That's that Iraq shit. We need someone like you around. *Commando*," the stranger joked.

After introducing himself as Kenny, and a brief conversation, Kenny assured officer Mcgurt that his son would be alright. Kenny seemed genuinely concerned and for some reason unknown he mistakenly believed that Mcgurt was in the military.

Upon Officer Mcgurt's request, Kenny was to call the police and explain the situation because he was the only other witness out there that night with a phone. He called earlier and they were already on the way Kenny explained.

Officer Mcgurt never shared the fact that he was a sworn cop. Sheiding his identity was normal, for security purposes. In addition to that Officer Mcgurt wasn't in the mood to talk, even tho he was a cop, just off duty and thereby responsible for the livelihood of this concerned civilian.

Officer Mcgurt tried the door with his hand. It was locked. Trying to spot his son from outside, he heard a car zoom up from the rear. To his surprise it was an officer on duty accompanied by his patrol car. His badge read McTaggart and he was responding to a shoplifting call. While briefing McTaggart on the robbery, Officer Mcgurt managed to hear loud gun shots. The sound effect was so loud that it reminded you of a block party.

Furious, Officer Mcgurt looked inside of the store. He saw a few hostages, laying on the floor, but still, no sign of his son. McTaggart was pacing nervously waiting for back up. McTaggart was just an inexperienced rookie so he wouldn't be much help anyway Officer Mcgurt concluded.

Officer Mcgurt looked inside to see if someone was harmed. But this ceased once more shots followed, directly behind him, only inches away. All of a sudden explosive gunfire appeared out of out thin air and was apparent: predominantly from the barrel of a 45-caliber hand-pistol.

Confused, Officer Mcgurt turned around only to see McTaggart's lifeless body drop to the ground. He could smell the fresh blood as it oozed down the officer's face. A bullet hole, four inches wide, was stuck right there in the center of the officer's forehead.

"Look Military boy. You seem genuine. So Imma spare you. But you aint *heard,* or *seen* shit. Understand?" Kenny threatened, as he removed the smoking gun from the officer's bowling ball shaped forehead.

"I said, do you hear me?" Kenny repeated, now pointing the gun at officer Mcgurt's forehead. After receiving a nod, Kenny confiscated Mcgurt's weapon and gave him a pat search.

"After you get your son ... *Leave,*" Kenny warned."

Following those words, two dudes busted out of the store. One of them held a hostage, a light skinned elderly woman, and she was crying. The poor old lady was scared to death.

Thinking back on his police academy training, Officer Mcgurt made an attempt to use the negotiation procedure.

"Please, don't do this man. That's somebody's mom. Let her go. Yall got the money. Nobody's here to arrest you guys. Especially not him," Officer Mcgurt pointed at the dead cop.

"Please," mcgurt begged.

After Kenny reassured Smoke that Officer Mcgurt wasn't a threat, Smoke lowered the gun and pushed the old lady to the ground. Shortly after he joined his accomplices in a blue van.

◆ ◆ ◆

Approximately twenty minutes later, Officer Mcgurt sat in front of a abandoned crack house spying on Kenny, the citizen/robber, and Smoke. They dropped the third assailant off and now they were in the middle of a very discreet drug transaction.

After making sure that his son was secured, officer Mcgurt hopped in his own car to pursue the suspects. Kenny never knew which car was his so he was able to trail them without raising any suspicion. Overhearing a phone conversation, Mcgurt glanced to the right and saw someone that caught his attention. It was Philo, one of the most infamous heroine dealers the city of Savannah had ever seen. Amongst the local precincts, Philo was rumored to be affiliated with the UAT—which was short for (Us Against Them), a secret society of organized crime. The organization was international stretching through the northern and southern regions of the Americas. It was even rumored that the group's influence was so strong that it was now moving into the Mexican cartel's territory. But those were just meaningless rumors as far as officer Mcgurt was concerned. Nothing more, nothing less.

Officer Mcgurt wanted to call for back up so they could film Philo commiting a crime in the act. But that would mean losing a visual on the two suspects, the ones responsible for tonights murderers, and he couldn't allow that to happen. He had to make this arrest. His plans for Philo was suspended. Until they were apprehended

All of a sudden, gun shots rang, out of nowhere, shattering Officer Mcgurt's car windows. Partial pieces of glass fell onto his skin. Mcgurt tried his best to dodge the rapid gunfire but he was unsuccessful.

Realizing that he was the target, Officer Mcgurt took a bullet to the chest. And shoulder, causing his broad shoulders to create a vertical position. Scared, he reached inside of his holster to retrieve the gun that he found on Officer McTaggart's dead body because Kenny had confiscated his during the search. But by then it was too late because the shooter was positioning the gun insde of Officer Mcgurt's face, therefore only seconds away from committing the third murder in less than 24hours.

Feeling like his chances of survival was better outside of the car, Officer Mcgurt leaped out, only to be outnumbered and surrounded by two teenaged boys. At this point Kenny and Smoke had come to investigate.

"Hol on, hol on, hol the fuck on. Kenny said, stopping the teens from murdering officer Mcgurt. What the fuck are yall doin'?" He asked, but before he could even receive a response, he figured it out. He stared at officer Mcgurt suspiously.

"Oh. You following us soldier boy? Speak up. I can't hear u Iraq? You twelve?" Kenny interrogated.

"He's the police. Can't you tell?" One of the youngsters' said never removing the pistol from out of officer Mcgurt's face. A massive amount of blood covered his entire body, smothering his attire, which consisted of a blue-collar shit, and levi jeans. Officer Mcgurt tried his best to explain but he only managed to cough up blood.

"Hun," Smoke uttered, handing some random smoker some heroine. The same product in which he just scored from Philo. Smoke wanted his drugs safe while he handled this situation. Kenny, you get his legs. Yall hold his upper body. C'mon yall. On the count of three."

Together, the four of them dragged Mcgurt's ridiculed body to the side of the crack house. There, Smoke, the person in charge, initiated his interrogation.

"You twelve?" He barked, accusing Mcgurt of being the police.

"Look's like a jack boy," one of the teens suggested.

After not receiving any response from Officer Mcgurt, Smoke raised the gun and pointed it in disgust as he played tug of war with his thoughts.

I knew I should've killt his' ass.

But before Smoke could pull the trigger he was interrupted. "Hold up dirty. After yall murk buddy, yall gon' clean up that blood? Because he wasn't following us. He was following yall's punk ass."

Silence

"This our hood. Now yall cool because yall OG'S. But if yall leave that body right there it's gon'be a problem."

The young thugs were now making demands from both kenny and smoke that caused minor tension.

After agreeing to the youngster's request, which included not leaving officer Mcgurt's body on the side of the trap house, smoke pulled the trigger, without any lack of haste or hesistation. Smoke fired additional shots, to confirm his assumption that Officer Mcgurt was going to die tonight. Then the duo dragged him to a nearby garbage disposal.

Together, they picked up Officer Mcgurt's body and threw it inside of the trash filled dumpster. The atmosphere was filled with shitty diapers and mildue.

"NOW THAT'S HOW YOU LEAVE A MUFUCKA STANKIN!" Smoke joked, as the dual stormed off in an abundance of laughter.

And that was the last thing that Officer Mcgurt remembered.

CHAPTER 3
New Allies

"Ladies and gentlemen. I have some breaking news. A man was shot and killed today after an attempted arrest. Our fox 28 news reporter Shannon Holmes has more on the story and is live at the scene. Shannon?"

"Thanks Dan. Just moments ago, Teddy Jenkins, also known as Smoke, was shot and killed by officers on this very porch. Witness's say Jenkins pulled out a weapon and wounded a detective during duty."

"Now sources say Jenkins was the man wanted for Monday night's double homicide, which included the killing of a cop, and a local store owner. No officers are available for questioning at the moment Dan but more details will be provided later tonight."

"My God. What a tragic event. This is very disturbing to the community."

"Sure is Dan. I agree."

Reading from the teller prompted camera, Dan, the news anchorman, moved along. In other news ...

Captain Dabruski walked towards Officer Mcgurt's hospital bed just as he was changing the news channel.

"Well well. Will you look at what we have here. Iron man," Cap joked.

"I see you saw the news already? So much for the surprise," Captain Dabruski sobbed.

"You just scared the hell out of me cap," Officer Mcgurt replied as his boss arrived inside of his hospital room unexpectedly.

"Sorry. My intention wasn't for you to be startled," Captain Dabruski apologized.

"So. How's it going? I see you made yourself comfortable. I may have to move my bed in here too. Looks relaxing. You mind?" Cap joked.

"Sure do."

"Of course u do. Were you always this stubborn?"

"Were you always a peeping tom?"

"Point taken."

They laughed at Cap's response.

"Clarissa left?"

Mhmm. Thank God."

"Is it that bad?"

"You don't know the half Cap."

"Sad. But if u say so. So I wanted to tell you what happened. That is, before the fuckin media did. But, Dabruski paused, shrugging his shoulders, I guess It's a little too late for that."

"Better late than never."

"Tell that to my wife."

Captain Dabruki continued after making that statement. "What the news failed to say is that both men were killed today, Wallace and Jenkins. The license plate number that you gave us registered back to a guy named Omar Jenkins. Omar was Teddy's, also known as Smoke's, older brother. Teddy and Dominque, who you knew as Kenny, took Omar's car without his permission according to him. He didn't know who the third suspect was," Captain Dabruski confessed.

Then Cap joined officer Mcgurt on the bed. He wanted to see Mcgurt's facial reaction once he reaveled this information.

"We located Dominique first. We found him standing on the

front porch at his sister's house in the Frazier Holmes projects. Before my officers could even identify themselves, he took off running. The drugs had obviously gotten the best of him, because he collapsed after a brief chase, Captain Dabruski paused, shaking his bald head. He got back up and started shooting. Sadly, he wounded two officers, which eventually lead to him being killed by SWAT," Cap informed regretfully.

"It took us a while to find Teddy. We gotta tip that he was in some gambling spot. So we waited until we had a positive I.D. on him before we made an arrest. But some kid blew our cover by yelling to his friends that we were the police. Because of this they scattered. Long story short we chased them. But some of our targets got away, and none of the ones that we apprehended matched Teddy's description. Anyway. After we prepared to leave, take a wild guess who shows up?" Cap asked pausing for a brief moment.

"Homicide detective Jackson tried to apprehend him, was met with confrontation, and a good ole' fashion bullet. And the rest was history. He left the scene in a body bag," Captain Dabruski explained.

After a brief conversation, Officer Mcgurt made his way to the restroom. Upon his return he sat back on his hospital bed in deep thought. His curiosity was getting the best of him. "Cap, I must've got shot a thousand times. I mean. It would be nice to know how I survived."

"Sure you wana kno? Because your going to die once you find out."

Officer Mcgurt nodded his head.

"Ok. Your funeral."

"I'm warning you, it's going to blow your mind. Hell I had to interview him three times just to satisfy my curiosity."

Seeing that officer Mcgurt's wasn't budging on his desire to know the truth, captain Dabruski looked in his eyes.

"Chris King. He saved your life Press."

"Nice joke cap. Didn't know you were a comedian."

"Seriously. He's the reason you're alive. Said he was in the area, needed to take a piss, and decided to do it behind that dumpster. He followed his intuition, looked inside of that trashcan, and found you there, nearly dead, Dabruski informed still surprised that Chris had a heart big enough to perform such a task. Hell, the medical examiner said that he even gave you mouth to mouth resuscitation," Captain Dabruski added, still in disbelief.

Officer Mcgurt just sat speechless. This couldn't be happening he thought, it just couldn't be. He hated dope boys. Couldn't stand them. As far as officer Mcgurt was concerned all dope boys could all die and the world would be a better place. They made a bad name for the black community. They were the main reason why white people considered blacks to be ignorant, worthless, and second-class citizens. And yet one of them displayed a sense of integrity and concern. How odd. This was ludicrous.

Drug dealer saved my life? O God. Why me?

After beating himself down, Officer Mcgurt fell into a deep state of unconscienceness. From that day forth officer mcgurt had no choice but to view drug dealers in a different manner. The fact of the matter was, somebody saved his life: *and that somebody was a heroine God that went by the nick name of Philo.*

CHAPTER 4
Just like my dad

Founded in 1733, Savannah was Georgia's oldest city. It also maintained the country's largest historic district, which was two and a half square miles. Over twenty cobblestones, huge southern mansions, plentiful gardens, quaint boutiques, and city parks with oak draped in Spanish moss. Savannah was a small ciy, but somehow, it managed to compete with the largest cities economically through tourism and e-commerece.

These were just some of the things that Mrs. Little was in the middle of sharing with her second-grade class. She was giving a history lesson and these were some things that she felt her students needed to know about their city.

"By a show of hands, how many of you guys ever been to the Oglethorpe mall? She asked, looking at two students in particular who were lost in their own conversation. A bunch of ME's and I DID's echoed throughout the classroom.

"It's named after General James Oglethorpe. He conquered the Spanish in 1742 for control of the entire State of Georgia," Mrs. Little informed.

Relaying her eyes on the two students, she pointed. "Mr. Thompson. And Mr. Mcgurt. Do the two of you mind sharing whatever it is that you're discussing with the class?"

Ignoring Mrs. Little, the two 2nd graders continued to laugh among themselves. "Preston. You wanna tell us what's so funny? Since you won't let me talk how about you do the honors?" Mrs. Little tempted.

Little Press stood up.

"A couple of days ago, me and my dad went to the store to get me some m & m's, skittles, and starburst. While we was in there some black elephant looking guy robbed it."

A few students laughed out loud.

"This other man made us lay on the floor, while the black elephant shot a man right in front of us. Chinese man," little press exaggerated, ignoring Mrs. Little. She wanted him quiet because he replied with a story that was causing an uproar.

The class laughed again. Louder. This time more kids joined.

"Mr. Mcgurt. I said that's enough. That's it. I'm calling your father. Again!" Mrs. Little threatened.

"And then his hat fell off. He had the ugliest hair cut I ever seen. He looked like a black pumpkin," little press joked.

"And when the lady laying next to me saw his head, he said, bitch, what the fuck you looking at? You aint never seen a nigga with a ugly hair-cut before, TURN YO'BALD'HEAD'ASS AROUND!"

The whole 2nd grade classroom burst out laughing in unison. Not one student was quiet.

Mrs. Little rushed out of the classroom. She left and headead to the principal's office because she could no longer tolerate the disrespect that was on display by *"Preston Mcgurt Junior."*

Family, friends, and a few law enforcement officers all gathered to celebrate Officer Mcgurt's promotion. The police department declared him a hero for his bravery. He was rewarded with a new ranking position and varies accomadations.

Still on the verge of recovery, two weeks passed in no time since officer Mcgurt was officially released from the hospital. Now, they were all gathered at his mother's house celebrating his epic return.

"Sergeant Mcgurt, Grandma Mcgurt teased him about his transition from a corporal to a Sergeant. Remember that surprise that I told you about?"

"Mmm-hmm", Mcgurt hummed, not really paying attention.

"It's on the way. Just got the call," Grandma Mcgurt informed.

"Grandma, Grandma, her twin grandchildren nagged as they bounced up & down. Where's your surprise?" the children complained. Grandma Mcgurt had been promising them a gift for weeks.

"It's coming. Now behave. And sit down."

The celebration was a success. Preston, the father, Clarissa, and some of their coworkers were in the middle of playing spades when the doorbell rang.

"Can you get that please?" Grandma Mcgurt asked her only son, preston mcgurt.

The person that stood behind the door was a complete shocker. He hadn't seen her in years. Standing five foot four, the chocholate stallion's appearance was flawless.

She look's good. Dayuuum.

"Long time no see—*Robocop.* Don't act all shy ni. Give yo' big sister a hug," Tandra greeted as the siblings embraced excitingly.

"Tandra. You look good girl. When did you come home?"

"Yesterday. Heard about the celebration and I wanted to surprise everyone," Tandra explained as she walked inside. She glanced at the gold chandeliers that dangled from the ceiling. Doing big things aren't we. Congratulations. Sergeant Mcgurt," Tandra teased mockingily, mushing his chest playfully with her index finger.

Everybody welcomed Tandra home after vacationing for three years. Initially, it started out being a party for Officer Mcgurt. But Tandra's presence overshadowed everything. Her return was unexpected and fulfilled the party's expectation.

Little press watched as Tandra tickled her twin children, Adam & Eve, his best-friends, and cousins. He couldn't remember the last time that he saw the duo this happy. This made him a little jealous. But ultimately, Tandra's return created a harmonious environment, so little press was looking forward to getting to know this mysterious lady better.

"Little press. Com'ere boy. Give yo' aunte a hug. The last time I saw u you had on spiderman drawers. Now you all grown n stuff. Looking just like your Dad," Tandra teased, as she pushed little press's chest playfully.

After being entertained for hours, the guest left. The celebration left all of the adults exhausted. The only people that remained were immediate family.

"So. Sis. What's your plan? I mean. In terms of employment?"

"Honestly. I'on know yet. I guess I'll find a job Monday. But I was really thinking about going back in school."

"Oh okay. If you want, you can use me as a reference."

"Really bro? You'd do that for little ol me? Thanks. Because a bitch broke ass hell."

"Tandra."

"Sorry ma. I meant, because a girl's broke as hell," Tandra corrected.

"Look Tandra, Officer Mcgurt blurted. Your my big sista. So I love you. But you gotta get it together. Mama too old to be taking care of *your* kids."

"Oh lord, here we go. Please don't start press here. I aint been home for twenty-four hours yet and you already starting with me."

"I'm just saying Tandra. This is the third time you went to prison. And every time you get out, it's the same speech. *Imma get a job, Imma go to school, Imma do better, blah blah blah.*"

"You too old for that Tandra. I hope you serious about things this time because those kids need a mother figure and mama can't keep ta--

"Fuck, you, okay. Pig! You just too dam dramatic for me! U got female tendencies. Is your period on? Ms, I need a tampon. Shit. All that yelling in my goddam ear."

"And FYI Imma convicted felon dumbass, so for me, discrimination is normal. And don't front like everythang's going good for you out here. People talk, even from prison. They sure do honey. I heard that you, Mr. big bad cop, was having trouble in paradise. What a shame. Now what u need to be doing is figuring out how u gonna' pay that overdue mortgage, that's what you need to be worrying about, instead of me n mind. Bills don't pay themselves boo boo."

"You're a poor excuse for a mother."

"And so are you, Preston Mctwerk. Heard you gotta pussie between those legs. Probably why you and Clarissa's beefing."

Sensing the hostility in the vicinity, Ms. Rebecca made an attempt to lighten the mood. She was Grandma Mcgurt's best friend for thirty years and universally accepted as family to the argumentative siblings.

"Adam, Ms. Rebecca chirped. Where does your name comes from?" Ms. Rebecca asked. He was busy fighting his twin sister over who would sit on Tandra's lap.

"I was the first man," he blurted

"And I was the snake," his twin sister hissed.

Everybody started laughing, including Officer Mcgurt and Tandra.

"No. I thought you let the snake trick you. Remember?" Grandma Mcgurt reminded.

"Mmm-Hmm. I let the snake bite me. *Nanna*," Eve blushed.

Everybody started laughing again.

Once everyone settled down some, Eve spoke up. Playing with her brother left her dizzy with an adreline rush and she had something that she wanted to share with the group.

"Grandma, Eve said out the blue. She was almost out of breath. When I grow up. I want to be just like mommie."

The whole room fell silent at that moment. They were all astonished. Even Tandra, and she was the one that birthed the devilish child.

Grandma Mcgurt always stayed out of Preston and Tandra's arguments. She loved them equally and often refused to pick sides. So most of the time she remained neutral. But this time she had to agree with her son. Her daughter was a mess. Statistically, the chances of Tandra changing were as slim as Whitney Houston when she performed during the Michael Jackson tribute. In the past, tandra was a drug dealer, thief, and prostitute, and old habits were hard to break. Tandra's future would be filled with violence, and havoc, especially if her self-proclaimed rehabilitation progress wasn't authentic. These were some of the thoughts that came from the female of the elder generation, the first member of their independent family tree.

Then there was her granddaughter, Eve. The little girl was out of control at a young age and already bad. Grandma Mcgurt just imagined what her granddaughter's future would contain. Eve's behavior condition was even worser than little press's and that boy was practically lucifer himself. The only difference was, little press had a positive role model for guidance, unlike his devious first cousin.

Grandma Mcgurt shook her head in disgust as she thought about the female branch of the Mcgurt dynasty. It was hard to stomach the fact that her legacy would be left into the hands of someone that idolized a criminal.

Sensing the awkwardness again, Ms. Rebecca smiled at little press. He never participated. He just watched from afar.

"And what about you baby. What are you going to be when you grow up? Hun suga?"

"When I grow up. I wanna be a police officer, little press smiled, proudly, as he poked his little chest out.

"Just like my dad."

15 YEARS LATER

CHAPTER 5
Blessings in disquise

Officer Mcgurt hopped out of his patrol car and made sure that he had the right address. After confirming his suspicion, he proceeded to knock on the door with caution due to the profanity that echoed throughout the entire neighborhood. An African American couple was in the middle of a heated argument and he had been sent to defuse the situation by the local authorities.

"Fuck you too then, bitch. Ratchet ass."

"I betchu yo' tongue like this ratchet ass doe' don't it? Shit mouth."

"You's a fuckin' bum Trick. Broke ass. The only thing you ever gave me was crabs."

After a brief knock from Officer Mcgurt, and his partner in training, Officer Davinci, the door swung open. Shortly thereafter a middle-aged woman revealed herself. She wore micro braids on her scalp which was covered with a bed bonnit.

"I HOPE YALL HERE TO GET HIS ASS! LITTLE DICK MOTHAFUCKA. JUST DO—

"Ma'am, ma'am, calm down, Mcgurt exclaimed. You don't have to yell ok. Now we're here because someone reported a domestic violence at this address."

Robe open, the woman stepped outside, looked across the street, and yelled to nobody in particular. "DUM ASS NEIGHBORS. ALWAYS IN SOMEBODIES BUSINESS. NOSEY ASSES."

Once inside, and after they managed to calm the woman down, Officer Mcgurt conducted an investigation. He had already scribbled the couple's names, occupations, and previous background's down on his notepad.

"Now. What's the problem?" He asked.

"Nuthin. Some broad talkin about we fucked. She's lying tho. On god," the man explained.

"Dirty-dick dog. Stop lyin."

"You retarded. I shouldn't've never ever ever ever fuck with you. *Bum bitch*," the man complained, pointing his frail fingers in her middle age face. The tension between the dysfunctional couple was rising and too explosive. Eventually, officer mcgurt's partner decided to intervene.

"Turn around," Davinci demanded.

After following instructions, the man was forced to place his hands behind his back. "And have some respect for this sista. See, that's the problem with you young punks. Too disrespectful. Your not so tough now are you? Cuz. Speak up blood? Thats what you are, right? One of those gangbanging idiots?"

"GET OFF OF HIM!" The woman shouted pushing Officer Davinci off of her boyfriend, causing him to fall violently. He stumbled on a nearby sofa.

Confused, Davinci lifted himself up and pulled out some mase. He tried to restrain and spray the womanbut his attempt came to a halt thanks to officer Mcgurt's reflexes. A choke hold prevented Officer Davinci from arresting the girl. But even this didn't restrict his anger which was on full display through a series of curse words and death threats.

Officer Mcgurt pulled officer Davinci outside to have a pep talk with him. The situation was getting out of hand, quick. Regretfully, He left the couple in the house unattended.

But his co-anchor was pissed. "Get the hell off of me Mcgurt! That's assault on a fuckin officer. Her ass is going to jail!" Davinci roared.

"Really? Assault on an officer? Last time I checked I was training you."

"Dammit Mcgurt, take your head out of your ass. Wasn't I defending her? Why would she attack me? Doesn't make any sense. See, that's the thing I don't get about women. They're fuckin idiots."

"I mean it Mcgurt. She's going down," Officer Davinci promised.

After numerous attempts, Officer Mcgurt finally convinced Davinci to drop the charges. This could potentially go to court and result in a pretty lengthy prison sentence for the female so Mcgurt felt sympathy to some degree. Soon, he went back inside. Davinci decided to remain outside which was a good idea officer Mcgurt thought.

Upon his reentry Officer Mcgurt noticed that the guy was in the process of exiting. The guy had clothes inside of his hands, which he was in the middle of stuffing in several suitcases, the entire time. The micro braided chick was dead on his trail and in a complete state of shock and disbelief.

"Have fun at your bitch house!" She yelled accusingly.

"I will," the guy replied sarcastically.

"And don't bring your punk-ass back to my house anymore. Matter-fact—while It's still on my mind--let me get my keys."

Ignoring her, the guy continued to leave, walking towards his car with the suitcases. Now that the police was called, there could never be any reconciliation. The line that was crossed today knew no limits. To this guy, the middle age chick's sin was unforgiveable.

"You refusing?" the middle age chick repeated, after receiving no response, knowing the police would have to intervene.

Knowing this, the guy complied, stubbornly, by tossing the keys to the concrete part of the pavement.

"Bum bitch," the guy mumbled again under his breath.

Officer Mcgurt watched the guy leave willingly. Usually, when he responded to a domestic violence call, he ended up taking someone to jail. But in this particular situation, there was no proof that any violence occurred. On top of that, the man hadn't refused to vacate the property, or committed a crime, so technically, the officers didn't have a legitimate reason to arrest him. And judging from the flow of things, it didn't look like that would change.

Or so he thought. The woman's next set of words changed the flow of the situation.

"Mmm-hmm. Yup. Leave then. I don't care. I got niggas lined up like a seven-eleven for "this" twat. Including your daddy. He's been wanting to eat me out for years. *Step-son.*

"So go ahead. You better run. Talkin about my pussy tired, boy bye. Your pockets tired boo-boo. And so is that little dick of yours."

"I hope you get pulled over too witchyo'dumb'ass. Riding around with all that dope. Yup. He sells dope yall. Don't just stand there and look stupid. What are yall waiting on? Christmas? Arrest his ass."

◆ ◆ ◆

Filling out a police report was always an aggravating process. Sometimes, the standard process could take as little as 30 minutes. While other tasks, took hours. And today's task was no exception.

After Officer Mcgurt showed Davinci how to fill out the police report, Davinci had to vacate the vicinity. Apparently, his eight-year-old son was in an accident and he had to get dropped off at the emergency room.

Officer Mcgurt thought back on his career. He'd been working at this particular precinct for three years now after graduating from the academy. He gained a lot of respect in his community for his part time work with handicap kids and backing nonprofit organizations. Assisting with the homeless and speaking to the youth were also some of officer Mcgurt's contributions to the empowerment of the black community. Officer Mcgurt was a philanthropist. But he had zero tolerance for those who broke the law. If you commited a crime, you were going to jail, no exceptions. Officer Mcgurt was the black sheep within the law enforcement community. His reputation for being an asshole succeeded his personality. But his heart was far-more pure than the public's perception.

Ordinarily, Officer Mcgurt would've took both parties to jail. But no crime was commited by the couple. At least not by the woman of interest. Marijuana and crack cocain was found in the possession of her male counterpart.

After the woman "snitched," the officers searched the guy's car, and sure enough, the guy was dirty. Minor drugs were discovered. Just enough to send him away.

Feeling guilty for searching the guy's car without a search warrant, Officer Mcgurt cut on the air conditioner. The man was sitting in the back seat of the squad car sweating. They were driving in the middle of traffic and only a few minutes away from the Chatham County Jailhouse.

"Say bruh," the guy said from the back seat. He hadn't said a word since they dropped Officer Davinci off.

"Look. I know you gotta job to do. And I'm not trying to step on no toes. But I need a favor. I need a cigarette. Bad. Ol girl got me *stressin.*"

"And you already know I can't smoke once I get to the county. Gotta pack on me rite ni," the soon to be jailhouse occupant begged.

"Please officer."

Once they got off on seventeen, the highway, to the soon to be jailhouse occupant's surprise, they pulled into a McDonald's parking lot. Parnanoid, Officer Mcgurt made sure that there were no witnesses, especially within his department. Then he hopped out, unlocked the door, and took off the guys handcuffs. Hesitant, he gave him a lite.

"Thanks, jailhouse replied, thankful that officer Mcgurt wasn't a jerk.

"And don't take my kindness for a weakness. Next time you won't be so lucky," Officer Mcgurt warned before heading back towards the driver's side of the squad car.

Tossing the cigarette bud to the ground, Mr. soon to be jailhouse reached for the car door handle. It was locked. This produced a sense of confusion and frustration.

Fuck's he doin? I'm ready to go to fuckin' jail

Jailhouse knocked on the window, signaling officer Mcgurt to unlock the door. But officer mcgurt did the opposite. He locked the doors and left. He disappeared.

Mouth hanging three inches from the ground, the ex, soon to be jailhouse occupant, watched as the squad car pulled out to ongoing traffic, disappearing in the midst of the white lines that separated the intersection.

"Salute," ex jailhouse mumbled to himself still in disbelief. Officer Mcgurt was a good cop in his book. And no one could tell him different.

"You know. We were about to kick your door down back there. You okay?"

"I'm sorry. I must've been giving my newborn a bath," Toni explained, as she placed the little boy on her lap preparing to spoon feed him. The baby was sitting in a high chair. Toni had a total of three kids, two of which sat watching cartoons.

"My boo boo ready to eat? Yes him is. Aint that rite boo boo?" Toni cooed to her newborn in her best impersonation of a baby's voice.

Mcgurt and Toni were in the middle of a conversation when Agent Love returned. "When's the last time you cleaned the house?" He inquired.

"Mmm. Last night. Why?"

"Something wrong?"

"That's what I'm trying to figure out Toni," Agent Love replied starring at Mcgurt who seemed to have formed a bond with the baby all of a sudden. Mcgurt was holding the baby's pacifier while making funny faces.

"Does Arkee sell dope?"

"Dope? Arkee? No."

"Are you sure about that Toni?" Agent Love was losing his patience.

"Of course. You think I'd have a drug dealer around my kids? How dare you," Toni snapped defensively.

"Honestly, I didn't until now. It's' funny that you say u cleaned up last night. Yet someone, presumably you, just cleaned the bathroom prior to our arrival."

"I was washing my baby when you guys showed up."

"In the toilet Toni? Come on. I do this for a living you know, and I'm good at what I do. First of all, that air freshener, or whatever that was that you just sprayed in there is stink. Smells horrible. Second, that bath-tub hasn't been used in days. There's no trace of fresh water in that tub, period. So your telling me that you just washed your kids without water? I know you don't expect me to believe that do you?"

"Are yall done? Because I have somewhere to be," Toni spat heading towards the door. Apparently, she was ready for the narcotic agents to leave. But Agent Love didn't get the hint.

"You flushed it. Didn't you?"

After not receiving a response, he continued. "How much was it? Two. Three. Four kilos? I hope you didn't flush four kilos of Arkee's dope Toni. Big mistake."

"Is this a joke? If so, you got me. Ha ha. Shits so funny I forgot to *laugh*."

"I was washing my baby earlier and yall can't prove that I wasn't," Toni defended snapping her neck and transforming into a ghetto diva all of a sudden.

"Mama, ma-ma, maa-ma, one of her kids yelled. They were still sitting in front of the television watching nickelodeon. I got to pee," the child whined.

"Alrite babie. Mama comin', Toni assured, watching her middle child as he held onto his private parts. Just hold it for mommy for a few more seconds' okay honey? I have to show these assholes to the door."

Having failed at finding any drugs, Agent Love decided to wrap it up. He gathered up all his agents and headed towards the door. "Look Toni. Arkee's a millionaire, running a part time operation from your home, where your kids lay their heads. If you care anything about your children, you need to cut your ties, I'm telling you right now. Because I can assure you, real soon, he's going down, like the titanic, it's just a matter of time. I know you thought that you were helping him by flushing that dope, which I know you did, regardless of what you say, but you weren't. In reality, you're just making yourself another one of our targets, which isn't smart. You're aren't willing to go to prison over Arkee's sin are you Toni? Dick dat good?"

Agent Love paused for a second to let the severity of his words sink in. "And you do know that the social service department would've took your kids, had we found anything? I don't know about you, but I'd lose my mind if the state took my kids. Shit, I got two babies. And I'd die before I let that happen. Just imagine your little man, the one that has to pee, in a group home, not a pretty sight. There, he'll have plenty of time to piss alrite. Piss big bubba, his bunkie, the fuck off for whining so goddam much."

"Get out while you can," Agent Love persuaded, reaching inside of his pants pockets. He handed her a business card. I got two words for you Toni.

"*Big bubba*," Agent Love reminded.

Not long after that took place, Officer Mcgurt found himself knocking on Toni's door alone. After he reached his squad car, he realized that the baby's pacifier was still inside of his pants from earlier. He had taking it accidently. But he had every intention on returning it.

Not receiving an answer, Officer Mcgurt invited himself in. Surprisingly, the door was unlocked. Entering the living room, he saw that one of the kids was still watching cartoons. Toni was still helping her little boy in the bathroom he presumed.

Placing the pacifier back on the baby's high chair, Mcgurt watched as the child let out a loud burping sound. At least they're being fed properly he thought. Some of the mothers that he encountered was just plain out trifling. Maybe agent love was wrong. Maybe Toni wasn't the lying bitch that he had said she was during their departure.

Reaching for her pacifier, the baby knocked it on the floor accidentally. He picked it up. There, he noticed that the baby was sitting on top of something suspicious. Whatever it was, it was being covered by a burgundy towel. From the angle where Toni stood, just moments earlier, it was unnoticeable, but her absence diminished the invisibility.

Curious, Officer Mcgurt tugged at the towel until its fabric no longer surrounded the object. Immediately he was shocked by his discovery. A fresh batch of cocaine revealed itself, ample amounts of it. The smell of the dope blended in with the baby's odor. Apparently, little man had just took a dump in his soft, shitty-diaper.

Immediately regretting giving Toni the benefit of the doubt, Officer Mcgurt thought about Agent Love's comment. Love was right. He was good at what he did. Love had given a accurate descrtiption of her deceptfullness. Toni flushed the dope. And she would've gotten away with it if it weren't for honest cops like him.

◆ ◆ ◆

Hours later, after the scene settled down, Agent Love pulled officer mcgurt to the side for small talk. They had been back and forth in the house for hours and they were in the process of finally wrapping things up.

"Nice job Mcgurt. I liked the way you followed up on your suspicion. You could've walked away when you saw that towel, but you didn't. You nailed that lying whore to the cross, Jesus style. You don't know how much of an attribute you were to our investigation on this Davis case. Thanks man."

"Just glad I can help. What'll happen to the kids? Only part I regret."

"Don't kno. We contacted her mom and she's on her way."

"Really? Child service's not going to interfere?"

"I doubt it as long as there's a living relative that's willing to accept them. I was just fuckin with her mind, that's all. You got to play mind games with these criminals in this business Mcgurt, you'll see. Why do you think she left that door unlocked?

Simple. Because I got inside of her head. That's why."

They discussed how much time Toni would get in prison. Agent Love promised that it would be a long time before Toni saw the streets again and also that her boyfriend Arkee was also being charged for the 3 keys of cocaine that they confiscated thanks to officer Mcgurt.

"Ever wonder what's it like in Narcotics?" Agent Love asked seriously, changing the subject.

"Or do you wanna write tickets your whole career?" He added, after not receiving an immediate response from Mcgurt.

"And what if I do?"

"But you don't. You hate it. It's written all over your face."

A few minutes of silence claimed the atmosphere before either spoke again. Then Agent Love broke the brief moment of awkwardness. "I think you'd make a great CNT agent Mcgurt. The pay is better, the hours are more flexible, and best of all, you wouldn't have to wear that tired ass uniform anymore. You could arrest a mufucka and still be fly like yours truly, Agent Love emphasized pointing to his own chest. There's no limit to the perks brotha. I'll tell you what. I like you press, that's what I'm calling you from now on. And like I was saying. Imma' talk to my boss *personally* on your behalf. That's how much confidence I have in you."

"So?" Agent Love asked with a huge smile on his big black face.

"I don't kno man. I need time to think."

"Sure buddy. Think it out. Just don't think too long. We got tons of more houses to raid."

CHAPTER 7

Long time' no see

Charlotte lifted up her very flexible limbs and opened up her legs in a pointed V formation. She curled her index finger and played with her clitoris as she licked her glossy lips. Moaning and panting, she moved her index finger into her soaking wet vagina. Then she and press's lips met, and they tongued each other in a passionate sensual kiss.

Overwhelmed by all the foreplay, press shoved her onto the bed and inserted his bulging shaft. Then he pushed her legs back to her ears as he rammed everything that he had inside of her.

"Harder baby. Mmm. That's rite. HARDER!" Charlotte screamed in ecstasy.

Press beat the pussy as if tonight was his last night on earth. Sweat poured from his face. But this notion didn't prohibit him from smacking pelvises with the woman that he loved.

Nearing an orgasm, Charlotte held on to Press for dear life. She started pinching and scratching his back, causing him to increase the intensity of his pace.

"Oooh. Oooo," Charlotte rejoiced, as her already satisfied body shook uncontrollably.

After their sexual encounter, Press sat on the edge of their colossal bed, that stood almost four feet tall. He was sweating like a Hebrew slave and he needed some air.

"So," press managed in between breaths. What do you think?"

"You were aiight. On a scale of one to ten—Uhh--I'd say five,"

Charlotte joked.

"Yeah, five plus five, don't play with me woman. You know my sex's the bomb."

"Boy bye," Charlotte replied rolling her eyes playfully.

They both burst out in laughter.

"Seriously doe bae. Did you think about what we just discussed? You ok?"

"Mmm-hmm."

"Nobody's sleeping in my bed is it?"

"No dru hill," Charlotte teased.

"I think you should take it."

"The narcotic's offer?"

"No the narcotic's offer. *Duh.*"

"Got somethin' for that smart mouth."

"Whatever sisqo. On another note, this is the reason we both got into criminal justice. To elevate our careers and fight crime. It's all we ever talked about in high school."

"I sure as hell don't plan on being a probation officer forever. I want my boss's job. Can't sit at the bottom long."

"Exactly," Press said as he reversed positions with her. Charlotte hopped on top of press but now his very exhausted body was on top of her. The rest of the night was filled with passionate sex following their discussion.

"Come on now Mcgurt. You're telling me that the CNT department wants to recruit you? But your hesitant? Am I hearing this correctly? Maybe I need a hearing aid. I dunno. That sounds stupid. There's nothing to think about. You make that transition Press. End of story."

"Just don't like answering to noone. I'm used to being the Chief of the village. Especially on my beat."

"And taking the job means giving all that up."

"All of what? You say it as if its a fuckin luxurious hotel re-treat or something? Jeez Press. With this salary, we're barely above the fuckin poverty line," Officer Daniels cursed. He was a trusted friend of officer Mcgurt and a fellow officer. They were on their lunch break and decided to get some glazed doughnuts at a local spot in the East Savannah area. Not wanting to argue any further, Officer Daniels decided to change the subject.

"Press. Twelve-o-clock."

"*Goodness gracious,*" Press mumbled in a trance like state of consciousness. There were two young women exiting the same building. They had just walked outside of the dunking doughnut spot carrying a box of doughnuts.

"Need help?" Officer Daniels was on a mission. If those women were drinks, he needed a cup, because he was too thirsty. 36-24-36 were the only numbers that seemed to come to his mind. The girl whom he spoke to had to be named Ms. Ass he thought.

"No. I got it," Ms. Ass reassured.

"You sure? Because you look like your about to have a hernia?" Officer Daniels flirted further.

"I'm sure," Ms Ass repeated, batting down Officer Daniels best pick up line. In her eyes police officers were stupid. They risked their lives for small salaries which was foolish. The police were a bunch of Tricks that wore ugly uniforms to match their ugly faces. Officer Daniel's was no exception to her rule. In fact, in her opinion, he was uglier than most.

Press watched as the two girls hopped in a candy apple Tahoe. The big body SUV was accompanied by 26-inch rims with sparkling gloss located on the outside exterior. The girls were balling harder than them and Press envied that to some degree. Starring at one of the girls, it was almost as if him & her had made eye contact for a second. It seemed almost as if he was visibly attracted to her and the feelings were mutual.

Does she like me? Press asked himself. The girl looked like a young Stacy Dash fresh off the cover of a playboy magazine.

What would she want with my broke ass? A honda civicdriving cop whose salary is so small that it could fit on her picky?

Press had to check himself for having these thoughts. He was tripping. Charlotte was all the woman he needed he concluded. She was no Stacy Dash, but she was real. And most importantly, his. Any day of the week press would take loyaly and authenticity over beauty and booty.

After Ms. Ass rejected Officer Daniel's advances for the millionth time, he finally got the hint and headed back towards the squad car. The lunch break was almost over. Officer Daniel's ended up showing Press some recent pictures of him and his wife at the Bahamas and they exchanged a few laughs and playful insults. Officer Daniels hopped inside of his squad car and proceeded to crank the vehicle. He was in a rush all of a sudden.

"What's the rush? Breaks not over. You wanna' arrest somebodie that bad? They must've wrote fuck the police on your car again?" Officer Mcgurt joked.

"Don't flatter yourself. While you were viewing my pics, my radio went off. There's a home invasion in process."

"Where?"

"Woodhouse apartments."

"Woodhouse apartments on the Southside?"

"Didn't I just say that press, dam. And no, you can't tag along. Its out of your district. Plus you don't know anyone out there."

"All true. Except for a couple in apartment 2A".

"That's the address."

Silence.

"Ok. Fine, don't believe me. But don't say that you weren't *fore-warned*," Officer Daniels threatened as he started the engine finally.

"Where're you going? You do realize that the Southside's not your beat right? Officer Daniels quizzed. But Officer Mcgurt couldn't hear him because he too busy starting his own vehicle and speeding off in a hurry.

◆ ◆ ◆

The drive to Woodhouse apartments took less than fifteen minutes. Being that Officer Mcgurt was out of his assigned district, he had to radio in to his superior to inform him of his whereabouts.

By the time they arrived on the crime scene dozens of black uniformed cops were already present. Some of them were prowling outside, some were investigating things from the inside, while others just stood at the front entrance of the house holding a conversation.

Inside, cops were scattered like roaches inside of a project building. Everything from dressers, to tables, even the furniture was being examined. A thorough investigation was taking place and it was obvious. Every cop in the entire city was there it seemed.

Heading towards the living room, Press saw Officer Jackson interviewing both of the alleged victims. Jackson was a fellow officer that Press met during his brief stay at the police academy. There, sat a guy whom looked to be around Thirty years of age, and a female who favored twenty-one ish. Press kept the conversation with Jackson brief, otherwise, they wouldn've gotten any investigative related type of work done. Officer jackson's mouth was like an engine with extremely low mileage: *It never stopped running.*

"Sup Mcgurt? Aint seen you in forever. Where you been hiding? The Bahamas? I know how yall fellas do at the 5th precinct."

"Been laying low."

"Sure you have. We need to link up for old time sake. You remember how much fun we had after graduation. Two male whores on a mission. So what a—

"Press," the female hostess greeted interrupting and embracing press urgently. She disregarded the fact that his co-workers were staring at the two of them unapologetically.

"Boi. You'n know how to text nobodie back? What's your Facebook name so I can send you a friend request?" the hostess asked, pulling out her phone openly. Press didn't want to draw too much attention so he kept it sweet and short. He reminded her that he was at work and also that this wasn't the setting for a reunion, party, or social media expedition. Press wanted their relationship to remain low-key even though the officers in the other rooms came into the living room curious to find out how he knew one of the victims.

Thinking fast, Press searched the area with his eyes. "Jackson. Mind if I speak to this young lady in private? Won't take long," he asked.

Once the coast was clear, and his request was granted, press let his guard down.

"You ok?"

"Sure."

"What happened?"

"Some niggas kicked in our door, tied us up, and took Tods shit."

"What they had on?"

"All black. One of them had on white," The hostess victim explained.

"What did they take?"

"Man, I aint seen you in faever and all you wanna do is ask a bitch about a robbery. Typical you. Hi press. I've been doing good for the last couple of months. Thanks for asking."

"I answered these interview questions like a millions times alreadie. I'm tired."

"I understand. I'm only trying to protect you."

"I know," the victim said, gently.

A moment a silence passed before another word was spoken. "Can I ask you a question?"

"Shoot."

"You didn't have anything to do with this did you?"

"*Robocop*," The hostress barked defensively.

"I'm sorry. It's just strange that you and Tod mysteriously gets rob the day after yall have an argument. And on top of that how does someone who robs people invade a house and only take from the guy? Females don't get a pass. Robbery suspects are normally sensitive to greed, not gender. Something's not adding up."

"And?"

"And If I find out that you're behind this incident, I'm arresting you, *personally*. You'll go down for being an accessory to a home invasion."

"Don't laugh, it's not funny. Think I'm playing," Officer Mcgurt threatened.

The hostess replied by lifting her birdie finger.

Then they conversed for a few more minutes before Press departed. Thinking back on their history together, press hopped back into his patrol car. He loved the hostess to death. But she was just too turnt up and lit. She had a nasty reputation for setting trapper's up to get robbed. Dope boys, jack boys, corporate guys, it didn't matter who the victim was to her. If you flaunted it, she wanted it, and it was just that simple. She had just gotten back to Savannah not even eighteen months ago from some out of town vacation. Nobody had seen or heard anything from her in five whole years prior to that. There was also a rumor circulating that she had varies contracts on her forehead. Press wasn't sure if there was any authenticity to those rumors. As far as he was concerned it was just word of mouth.

Thinking back on the incident, press read the verdict inside of his head. Guilty. On all counts. Without a doubt the female victim was responsible for what transpired. The robbery had her name written all over it.

Meanwhile, Officer Jackson was running his mouth as he re-read the information that the couple provided. He looked at every detail and realized that something was missing.

"Torrance," Officer Jackson pronounced, rereading the police report.

"It's Tod."

"O. Ok. Tod. What did you say your girlfriend name was again? I'm sorry. I'm terrible with names."

"Eve, Tod mumbled irritably as he picked up his cell phone and dialed a certain number.

"Eve Mcgurt," Tod repeated.

CHAPTER 8

Parents just don't understand

"Son. When's the last time you spoke to your father?"

Clarissa asked her only son. Press usually attended church with his mom on Sundays which was followed by a home cooked meal. Today was one of those days. After church, they fed their bellies. Now they were in the middle of a very intense conversation.

"I don't know, Press replied shrugging his shoulders. Probably last week sometime. You?"

"Now you know better."

"What? Yall can't have a conversation?"

"Not without arguing we can't."

"It never stopped yall before."

"Well. It should've," Clarissa cooed regretfully.

"I'm just saying ma. I'm so used to yall being together. It just hasn't felt right since yall decided to get a divorce."

"Preston Nathaniel Mcgurt Junior. Leave it alone."

"Is me talking about pops' dat hurtful? Because you calling me by my middle name. You only do that when you mad."

"Preston, you're acting like this all happened yesterday. It's been *over* five years since we split."

"I know ma bu-

"Boy that chapters closed, been that way for years. So don't come around here picking at no old wounds ya hear. Every time you come over here you' starting trouble," Clarissa threatened, clearly irritated at this point. Not wanting to push his mom's buttons, he switched subjects.

They talked about his girlfriend, Charlotte. They also talked about her new boyfriend and how nosey her neighbors were.

"So you really think that I should take the job ma?"

"I think you should do whatever makes you happy son. Misery costs a fortune. But happiness, now that's priceless. Nothing on God's green earth should jeopardize your serenity."

After the pep talk, press made his way to the door. He loved his mom to pieces and he valued her opinion because she always spoke from the heart.

"O, and before I forget. Your aunt Tandra called. She wants you to call her. Says it's urgent. Whatever that means," Clarissa informed sarcastically as she picked up the remote control and flicked the television to watch CNN.

◆ ◆ ◆

The young thug got off the bed and crawled up to Tandra's awaiting vagina. Once there, he began to lick it, and move his right finger concurrently in a circular motion, just like she had taught him too. Tandra moaned in pleasure. The youngster kissed her on her inner thighs as his mouth descended further down south, while inserting his right finger deeper and deeper inside of her love-box at the same time. Breathing like her body contained extra portions of oxygen, Tandra rocked her body back and forth, in an attempt to throw it back, making love and humping the young boys soaking wet finger. Aggressively, he lifted tandra's legs above her head. Then he licked and bit her butt cheeks while still fingering her. Without inhibition, he licked the middle of her butt. He then rolled her onto her stomach until the bigger part of her belly was flat. Anxious, the young fella primed himself up, gripping his already swollen loins, aiming to please Tandra's much older body doggy-style and condom less. The youngster pulled her hair and smacked her on the ass as he gyrated harder, longer, and faster.

"O. Fuck me. Com'on baby. That's it, teach mommy a lesson. She's been a really bad girl," Tandra's loud rant's echoed throughout the entire house. The sound of her voice was so crunk that she'd put little John and the East side boys to shame.

"That's rite. Don't stop baby. DON'T STOP!" Tandra begged, grabbing the sheets and biting into the pillow all at once."

After their orgasms were fulfilled, they were both exhausted and needed to take a break. The young boy was the "truth" Tandra thought. Where he lacked in age he made up for it in the sex department.

"Bae. What are you about to do? Because my nephew's coming over. We're going to a party," Tandra lied. She hadn't planned anything in advance. She just wanted to rid herself of the youngster immediately after having an orgasm.

"No, you're not," the youngster promised as he left the bathroom butt naked. He went to clean himself up shortly after their escapade. Tandra had her clothes halfway on at this point. But she was still in the process of getting dressed.

"What did you just say?" The youngster asked, trying to make sure that he heard her correctly as he made an attempt to grab her legs.

"I said, I'm going to a party. I know you heard me the first time. You're not deaf."

Ignoring her request, young blood continued.

"Boy stop. Unt-un, she said playfully. Dam, I'm losing my self-control? Tandra thought provocatively. My nephews on the way. You have to leave," she convinced fictitiously.

They wrestled back in forth for a couple of minutes, neither willing to compromise. For the moment anyway. The further Tandra's pants slide down, the less she protested.

After a series of attempts, the youngster finally managed to pull the pink thongs that Tandra had on to the side. Desperate, he inserted his tongue inside of her well-kept garden. Rotating his tongue in a circular motion, he nearly drove her crazy, causing her body to squirm & wiggle. He then used the tip of his tongue to enter further, encompassing the wall's located inside of her pussy and focusing on his main goal: *the clitoris.*

Tandra's candescent like body started to produce fruit full juices and countless moans. Her cries started to take on a completely different identity, matching the rhythm of his thrust's and her own hip rotation.

"You're not going anywhere," he repeated, this time aloud, inbetween his advances, confident that his head game was the best.

He's rite. His teenage tongue has me sprung. I can't leave. I'm a cougar.

Besides, Press wasn't about to come anyway. But she was, and that's all that mattered. Yeah, Tandra was definitely about to come alright, she thought, in the middle of their sexcapade: *right there on the young cubs lip.*

◆ ◆ ◆

Preston Mcgurt Senior, the father, had a career that represented the epitome of honor. His career was radiant and magnificent. From arresting some of the city's most feared criminals, to shaping the careers of varies officer's, Preston Mcgurt, the father, did it all to protect the integrity of the local law enforcement community. He built a reputation based on his loyalty, devotion, bravery, and zero tolerance model, just to name a few of his post-police-academy-graduating accolades.

Within the local region, notably the coastal empire, Preston

Mcgurt Senior had earned himself the most powerful position within the executive branch of the local judicial system. His ability to network and efficiently communicate with the urban community helped him elevate, and even gain the most successful businessmens trust. Through his social association, and intellect, Preston Mcgurt senior was able to establish power and the most effective political ties.

Press's mom, Clarissa, was no longer apart of Preston Mcgurt senior's life. To him, she was apart of his past. The no nonsense attitude and track record earned him the support of the city's biggest taxpayer's and voters. In just 22 short years on the force, somehow, he became the most significant figure within his jurisdiction.

Answering directly to the mayor, Preston Mcgurt Senior was a proud father of a cop and the current Chief of Police.

After ringing his dad's door bell, and a brief greeting, the Chief led Press inside of his house into his estate. The proper arrangements were made and the Chief took a day off so they could chat and update the status of their lifes amongst one another.

"I see you got yourself a maid? About time. This house is usually a mess."

"Who's the lucky lady?"

"How do you know it wasn't a guy?"

"Come on pops. You're my blood. You and I are one. We act, talk, and think alike. And I'm telling you this. No-one with a penis is ever cleaning my house. That's for sure."

"Point taken. Chanel Garcia's her name."

"Sounds like she's Mexican. You dirty dog lol. Hold on. Chanel Garcia. That name Sound's familiar."

"The news Anchor?"

"Rite. A Mexican news Anchor. You dirty, filthy, dog. Lol. I'm jealous."

"Why'd you wait so long to say something? Don't tell me. I get it. You knew that my handsome looks and boyish charm would be irresistible? That's why you haven't brought her around? Makes sense. I tend to have that effect on beautiful women. I make grown men insecure," Press teased.

"Don't flatter yourself son."

"You hittin dat'?"

"Inquisitive aren't we mr. irresistible. Odd characteristic for someone who claims to be God's gift to women."

"I'll say this, the Chief returned, propping his leg up in an effort to relax on his recliner. I run things around here. But in the bedroom--- Unt un un, he shook his head. The Chief remembered in a lustful manner as if he were in the middle of a sex session with her in that very moment. "She calls the shots."

"It's like that?"

"It's like that."

"Dayuum lol," Press joked.

"Same thing I said."

"So what's new son?"

"Everything. I just got off the phone with your crazy-behind-sister. She's psychotic."

"How so?"

"Ok. So first, she calls mom, apparently mad because I never return her calls. Second, when I finally do call, she starts talking about she wants me to bring her a gun. Un-fuckin-believable."

"So I politely reminded her that I was the police. I assured her that it wasn't gon' happen."

"And to make matter's worst the whole time that we we're on the phone she's *moaning*. Like someone's fuckin' her brains *loose*," Press complained in utterly disbelief. Again, she needs help dad. The psychiatric kind," Press repeated.

"What did she need the gun for?"

"She claims someone robbed her."

"For what? Crack-pipe?"

"Same thing I said," Press joked.

They both shared a brief laugh before Press continued. "Anyway. I just seen mama. She asked about you."

"Son. Stop it."

"No pops for real."

"So what's new?" The Chief repeated changing the subject. This was obviously a sensitive topic.

"I have a job opportunity with the Counter Narcotics Team."

Examining this information in his mind, the Chief grabbed the remote control and cut on the flat screen television.

"So you're not going to respond? Wow. I thought you'd be proud."

"I don't have anything to say press. Other than the fact that I think its a terrible idea. Why aren't you interested in the position that I set up for you?" The Chief argued, clearly irritated.

"Dad. Do we have to go through this every time?"

"Yeah yeah. I know. You want to make a name for yourself without my help and political connections. I get it."

"So then you understand. Why're you being so negative? You don't think I have what it takes?"

iSilence.

"I know you don't. You don't have to say it. And honestly, I'm offended. Your comments, and the lack therof, is fuckin' disrespecful," Press complained defensively, the pitch of his voice rising.

"Ok. Do you really want to play this game son? Fine, let's do it. I know that you've probably broken a few laws as a regular cop. I mean, after all, everyone does it. It's like that now, and it was like that when I was a rookie. So I get bending the rules. That make's sense."

"But what doesn't is you wanting to be a CNT agent. Son. These guys don't just break the law. They make them. And there's consequences for those that think that they're above the law, be it regular civilians, or those apart of the law enforcement community. Criminals are criminals in my book and they all go down eventually. Hell, there's hundreds, if not thousands of narcotics agents that're being investigated by the Internal Affairs as we speak, and they report their findings to *"me."* Matter-fact, my secretary just placed six different cases involving corrupted cops on my desk earlier this morning. Four of them will lose their jobs. The other two agents are being prosecuted for conspiracy."

"But at the end of the day, you're a grown man junior. So you'll make your decisions *with* or without me. But always remember. When shit hits the fan: *turn on the AC,*" the Police Chief cautioned.

CHAPTER 9
Public service announcement

The breeze migrated its way through the sky fluently. Birds could be heard flying, and chirping, through the air effortlessly, overpowering the two-mile radius the silence proclaimed.

Forsyth Park was one of the city's oldest parks. It was a place to be free for some, a playground for others, and the city's largest historical park in the urban community. But on this particular day it was quieter than usual, shockingly deserted, and a scapegoat for this particular law enforcement employee.

Contemplating his next move, Press fiddled with the mobile device that sat on his lap, which was filled with new cigarette buds, and pictures. Press was now sitting on a bench. He thought about his dad. Two weeks had passed since he offered his advice and now the discouraging words of his father was starting to registered inside of his head. His dad, the Chief of police, was right. He wasn't CNT material. He wasn't the kind of cop that kicked doors in with assault rifles and chased trappers. He was just a normal cop that had a fondness for enforcing the law, nothing more, nothing less. Was he really ready to step outside of his comfort zone? Probably not. This job would succeed his rational way of approaching criminals, one that would require more intelligence and courage than he currently possessed.

After battling himself with these thoughts, Officer Mcgurt punched a certain number in on his keypad. Then he let it rang. The receiving party answered on the 3rd ring.

"Speak."

"Sup bro."

"Who dis?"

"It's me. Press."

"You got thirty seconds to identify yourself. And ten of' dem gone."

"Agent Love, it's me, Officer Mcgurt. I helped bring down Arkee. Remember? Press assured, unfamailar with Love's jamacian accent."

"Press? Dat you? I didn't recognize the voice. Forgive me for the confusion. My family's from the island."

"What took you so long? Then again. Forget I asked. We don't have time to chit chat."

"I spoke to my boss about you and he's onboard. So I'll email the packages. Whats the address?"

"I didn't say I wanted the job."

"You're full of shit Press. You wouldn't be calling if you weren't interested. So what's the address? Do you have a Gmail or Yahoo account?" Agent Love repeated.

Then they had a brief conversation before ending the call.

From that day forth, press made a promise to himself to re-adapt to a new environment. Press was like a politician. He took his job serious and was widely known for his profession-alism and having a straight shooter type of personality. And while his characteristic traits wouldn't change, his career had to in order to flourish, there was no doubt about that. The sea-son's changed, so why couldn't he? He asked himself silently. Hell, even bobby brown managed to evolve somehow and he was pratically smoking crack all of his adult life.

Change was to become press's best friend. It wasn't just a phrase. It was more like a covenant that he made with himself. A covenant that he made privately, by telling Agent Love that he'd be happy to join the Counter Narcotics division.

Today was Officer McCourt's first day in the field as an active agent. Agent Mcgurt was the way that he was to be addressed from that day forth. Proudly, he practically praised his new-found job description.

"Narcotics Agent Mcgurt. Sounds good."

As press approached the building surrounded by unmarked cars in the parking lot, he thought about his near future. Two weeks had passed since the day that he agreed to take the job. Today, it was time to show and prove.

Entering the building, press saw pictures and frames of president George Bush Junior, J.Edgar hoover, and other influential Caucasian figure's throughout American history dominate the wall. There were several rooms, most empty. Others contained coffee tables, microwaves, and empty churches chicken boxes full of left-over skin and bones.

"Ranger. This is the man that I was telling you about. This is Preston Mcgurt. He's one of the good ones. Press. This is my boss. Captain Ranger," Agent Love introduced, brokering a relationship between press and his employer. Then they exchanged mutual handshakes and a few compliments. The old Caucasian man looked Press in the eyes and instantly became attached.

"How are you son? Been hearing a lot about'cha."

"Good things?"

"Are you kidding me? This guy here, Captain Ranger said, pointing to Agent Love. This guy right here has all the right connections. He's the modern-day Jesus. Think of it this way. If he recommends you here, you must be an angel," Ranger joked.

"Which means your God?"

"In the flesh, the old man boasted proudly with a serious look on his face."

"Son. Welcome to heaven."

They went over what the job required next. Captain Ranger informed Press concerning his responsibilities, roles, and limitations. Press was to work under the authority of Narcotics Agent Love, his superior, and boss.

After explaining this to press, Captain Ranger poured himself a cup of coffee. He was excited because presswas the missing link.

"So when do I start?"

"That depends," Ranger returned, taking a sip from his cup.

"On what?"

"Depends on your tolerance. And *availability*."

CHAPTER 10

Be careful what you ask for

Hours later, press found himself sitting in the backseat of an unmarked vehicle. The car was a crown victorian model, pitch black, minus the sirens. He was in the middle of training and being briefed on the city of Savannah's drug trade.

"Snitches are the lifeblood for agents like us Mcgurt, don't ever forget that, Agent Love explained from the driver's seat. Without them, we wouldn't have a fuckin clue."

"Thank God for snitches!" Another agent cheered from the backseat.

The other agents cheered in unison.

"Right there, Agent Love informed, pointing at one of the streets as they passed by slowly. That's where a looota activity goes on at. Constantly."

"Lot of idiot's in those dope' houses," Agent Jones interjected from the passenger's seat. He was Agent Love's right-hand man.

"Brillant. You guys "*know*" for sure that they're selling dope, daily, like you just said. But you're not doing anything to stop it. Am I missing something? Let me guess. They get a pass because they're snitches," Press theorized.

"Smart man. But we're not thinking about them fifty pack selling mufuckas. Ninety percent of them can't even afford a car, and that's just pathetic, especially for a hustler. Taking a mufucka to jail that sells dope and makes minimum wage's a waste of time."

"Besides, every time we lock one of them up, they just get right back out and post up on that same roach infested porch. *Aint nobody got time for dat.*"

"Bigger fish to fry," Press blurted, more so as an accusation than a question.

"Ah-ha. You learn fast."

Silence.

"Forget about the trappers? We target the kingpins?"

"Look at you, using the hippest lingo, I'm appalled. Most cops still live in the dinosaur age. They think a trap comes with cheese and mice. But to answer your question, basically. Why? Got a beef with us?"

"Fuckin' rite. Those guy's miswell hang a sign up that says, "Hey, look at us, We're selling dope, fuck the police," Press complained in a state of disbelief. He just couldn't believe that these cops would allow this type of blatant disrespect to go on.

The remaining three agents all burst out in laughter, causing press to wonder what was up with the sudden sense of humor. Then it dawned on him. This group was intoxicated. And out of control.

"Naw, Agent Love breathed, in between laughs. You know what press, I like you. You say what's on your mind. Another mufucka would've bit his tongue. Especially on his first day."

Agent Love spun the car down Augusta Avenue, targeting the West Savannah area. The mean mug's that came from the crowd of hustlers didn't go unnoticed.

"Seriously' doe. I understand where your coming from brotha. You think I don't want to ride down there and tear' dat' shit up? I do, badly, don't get me wrong. I just been around long enough to know that taking pettie criminals to jail isn't going to solve anything. If anything, it'll make matters worse."

"How?"

"Because snitches will stop bringing us the big fish. As long as they're rewarded for their cooperation, they'll roll over, even on a broke criminal. In addition, kingpins are almost impossible to touch without a snitch. Lower level drug peddlers are easily accessible. So a bust is a bust, big or small as far as they're concerned. What'll they care."

"So we hunt down people like Arkee. Remember him?"

"You'll get the hang of all of this buddy. After all, it's your first day, Agent Love said taking Press's silence as his cue to continue. You were born for this job press. I feel it in my bones."

Agent Love made a right and cut down the radio.

"O, and fellas, make sure you get enough sleep tonight. We got a long day ahead of us."

"On another note. Jones. Run in this store up here and get us some blunts. Diamond swissers. And a bic lighter."

◆ ◆ ◆

The following day at work was a much more exciting day. Today, they were more assertive, active, and hands on. They were currently in the process of frisking a young trap boy. The CNT agents outran the kid and had him hemmed up.

"C'mon. Why yall always fuckin' with me. That's not my shit dirtie," the boy complained.

"Sure it isn't," agent jones replied as he handcuffed the youngster. The kid sported an all-black dickie overall jumpsuit with matching dreadlocks. Press was busy patting down one of the kid's coconspirators during this time. To his surprise, he found some weed.

"How much was it?"

"Not much. Maybe an ounce."

"Then search his crybaby-ass again. Slick bastard. There's more where that came from. I'd bet money on it."

After giving press these orders, Agent Jones counted the money that he confiscated from his suspect. He smiled proudly after determining how much it was.

"How much money did you have homie?" He asked.

"You mean how much do I have? That's what you better mean. And I aint yo homie neither. Pussie."

"Whatever. How much?"

"Eight bands."

"You sure?"

"Dam right, you got me fucked up. I know how much bread I got, pig."

Spotting Agent Love from a distance, the kid called him over. Everybody in the hood knew that Agent Love was the one in charge and the trappers often used that to their advantage.

"What's up little homie?" Agent Love greeted as he approached the young dope boy.

"I need to holla'at'cha. Alone."

Realizing what the boy was requesting, Agent Love dismissed his agents thereby speaking to the adolescence trap boy in private.

"Big dog. Wad up wit dese punk ass narcs?"

"Same o same. You know how it goes."

"Naw, I don't. Enlighten me."

"*Hypothetically*," if my agents were to ever tell me that drugs were found in your possession, you go to jail. For years. End of story."

"If."

"No ifs."

"Not even "if" I know who just bought 10 bricks?"

"Who?"

"I thought you said n-

"Fuck what I said. I aint got time to play games with your little ass, Agent love snapped. Now either you' gonna' tell me or you can go' to' jail *bloodcot pussie' boi.*"

After the kid ran his mouth like the bitch that he truly was, and being intimated by love's jamacian accent,which he only used when he was upset, Agent love gathered up all of his agents and they prepared to leave. "Where's the drugs?" He inquired.

"Over there," agent Anderson pointed, as he shortly retrieved it for their team leader. After jones handed the trapper's dope over to agent love, he examined it. Then he shoved it inside of his pants pockets. No-one else seem to notice or even care for that matter. Except press.

"Good job press. Found somethin else?"

"Just the weed."

"Congratulations. This is your introduction, bigtymer. Manny fresh. Help him fill out the police report," Agent Love joked.

"He's a better man than me. All that boring' ass paperwork, behind a quarter ounce of weed? Not me. I'd set him free," one of the agents objected.

Press proceeded as instructed but with conflicting thoughts.

Maybe I should let this guy go? They're right. But then again, maybe this is a test. No, this guy's definitely going to jail. Doesn't matter how much weed's involved.

"Jones. Let the other kid go, Agent Love ordered. Thanks to him, we'll have a very interesting assignment tomorrow." Smiling after hearing these words, and being released from handcuffs, the young trapper gave agent jones the middle finger. Agent jones was trying to steal his money he reasoned. By

Georgia law, if you were caught in a well-known drug area with large sums of cash, your financial calculations had to be precise, otherwise, you were just making a donation to the police department, and the young dealer/snitch was smart enough to know that.

"You were right buddie. The dope wasn't yours," agent jones pronounced sarcastically. In Agent Jones's mind, he hated to give the foul-mouthed kid a break. But orders were orders.

"Hol on. You forgot' somethin'," The boy pronounced.

"My bad, Agent Jones replied. Taking his time, he reached inside of his pants pockets and handed the boy the pocket knife that he confiscated earlier as well. The color of its body was royal blue.

"Don't hurt nobody *cuz*," Agent Jones antagonized.

"Fuck the knife. Where's my money?" The young dope boy was visibly pissed now flare steaming from the inside of his nostrils

"What money? I don't remember you having any money. How old are you son? Fake-teen? You to young to have amnesia," agent jones joked as he made his way to a nearby undercover car.

"Now get the fuck away from my car before I get mad Craig. This my bike now punk, the thiefing narcotics agent said, mimicking Dee-bo on Friday, as he slammed the car door in the young trapper/snitch's face.

◆ ◆ ◆

In no time weeks passed since the first day press was introduced to the festivities of the counter narcotics division. For the past two weeks, he and his squad members were just doing normal protocol. A few searches, raids, and pat downs. A few criminals selling, bailing, and telling, the usual. Press was slowly losing his sanity. His co-workers were starting to become more and more unpredictable. This made him uneasy and not sure if this was all a test.

"All this time. You the one that's been dating Charlotte's fine ass. Do you know how long I been trying to hit that? I'm jealous."

"*Lol.* Seriously. I grew up with your girl. No bs. Back in middle school. She dated my cousin."

Counter Narcotic Agents Love and Mcgurt were riding alone on this particular occasion, just the two of them. They were on the way to see one of Agent Love's "mastersplinter's" as he liked to call them. Which was code for confidential informant.

"Press, Agent Love said after a few minutes of silence. Look. I know that eventually, you'll want a promotion. You baby face lookalikes always do. But promotions depend on connections, connivance, and politics. If you wanna get ahead in this life, you need a hierarchy. And I oversee the Indians. I'm the Chief of this village."

"Don't look so mean Press. I'm not trying to bust your balls here. The only that I'm trying to inspire you to do is be cool. And do your job. Nothing more. Complete that and you'll be aiight. Charlotte's my home girl from way back. And any friend of hers, is automatically a friend of mines. By default," Agent love assured.

The meeting with the mastersplinter was brief and to the point. After a few handshakes, sensitive information was provided, notorious names were given, and the "narcs" were on their way.

After they drove down a couple of blocks, press adjusted the knob on the radio. Lowering the volume, he sat up abruptly.

"What was that?" He questioned.

"You don't like rap? That was 2pac."

"You know that's not what I'm talking about."

"Mcgurt. That was some vital information. We needed that."

"So you gave him dope for it? I mean. What the hell's going' on' around' here? And don't deny it either. I saw you. I mean. Who are the real criminals here? Because at this point I just don't know anymore," press shrugged, raising his voice a tad.

"Sacrifice brotha. Sacrifice."

That response made press roll his eyes.

"And those were the same drugs that you took from that kid weeks ago. You k-

"Look, I know you didn't expect all of this to happen before you took this job I get it. But don't tell me how to do my job anymore mothafucka. Understand?" Agent Love barked, cutting press off.

"Either you adapt, or take your scary ass back to the 5th precinct! Love snapped. Who got u this job? Who put more money in your pockets? Me, that's who! If you gotta problem with the captain's method of running this ship then VAMOOSE MOTHAFUCKER!" Agent Love shouted. He nearly ran over a black cat while he was screaming these words.

Immediately feeling guilty afterwards, Agent love thought about his behavior. Press was honest. And a good cop. This was rare in the criminal justice field So leaving the wrong impression was something that Love didn't intend to do.

"My bad bro, agent love confessed. I aint mean it like that. It's just that, you gotta know that we're on the same team. And don't think for a minute that we aren't. Just try to understand where I'm coming from press. That's all I ask."

Seeing that he had press's undivided attention, Agent Love flicked his blinker and made a sharp left turn. Then he lit a Cuban cigar. "See. We can't use our badges but to a certain extent. When we're dealing with kingpins, and drug lords, we gotta use our street smarts to stay ahead of the curb. Do you think that these dope boys are dumb? I hope not. Don't under-estimate them. Running a successful drug operation isn't for morons. These motherfuckers out' here are einsteins. See, at the end of the day, it's just a business, like everything else. The only difference is that they're not under the radar. So they have more privacy. And less scrutiny."

"We have to be wolves in sheep clothing. These badges repre-sent the sheep. But we have to pull the wolves out of our inner-selves. We dam sure can't catch'em being sheep," Agent Love continued to preach.

After letting his words marinate for a minute, he continued. "Look man. All I'm asking you to do is tough it out a little, that's it. I'm not asking you to become a criminal, sell drugs, or to do anything that's' gonna' make' you uncomfortable."

Confused, press continued to stare out of the window like he had been doing for the pass thirty minutes. He finally figured it all out. This wasn't a test. This was chaos. On steroids x 2.

At this point, he couldn't help but think about his dad's advice. Press could only muster the strength to ask himself one ques-tion while meditating.

What did I get myself into?

CHAPTER 11

Snitches, get stiches

"Sweetheart. Wait. I got it."

"Are u sure?" Charlotte asked her co-worker, Pat, from the driver's seat of the government funded unmark car.

"Positive," Pat replied, as he pulled out his money preparing to pay for their meal. Just then they pulled into a fast food restaurant drive through.

"How much did you say the total was again?" Pat asked.

"Mmm. Hold on," the cashier said with much attitude as she looked at the total cost again. She cursed inside of her head.

Why is he taking so long to give me the goddam money? Shit. I'm ready for break.

"Twelve ninety-five," the cashier replied, with more attitude than the first time.

"Thanks, greeted Charlotte as Pat handed Ms. Attitude the money. Once they pulled off, Pat fastened his seatbelt.

"So where' are we going?"

"O. Well. I'm not sure about *"we."* But I'm heading to pay one of my parolees a visit."

"Where?"

"Utah Street."

"Good. I have one that I need to check on from around that area too. He better be home, Pat threatened. Do you have your equiptment with you? Because Immadefinitely be collecting a urine sample."

"I thought I was taking you back to the office?" Charlotte interrogated, as she made a sharp right turn.

"You are. After I collect the urine sample."

They rode in silence until they neared their destination. A brief conversation was exchanged between her and Press over the phone in the meantime.

"So when can you and I hang out?"

"I dunno."

"How come?"

"Because I don't."

"Did press ban you from having male friends?"

"Yup. Sho'll did."

"So what. We can flirt on the job, and talk during break, but we can't have a friendship outside of work? *Wow.*"

"I didn't know that having a friendly conversation with a co-worker during work hours was considered flirting. But Thanks. From hear on out I'll be sleep during break."

"Stubborn bitch."

"Pat, don't go there."

"Why not. U did. But I get it. Your too good for me now rite? I'm not some big shot narcotics agent so you won't give me the time of day," Pat flared in frustration.

"What's dat? You ready to go back' to the office? I got chu."

Pat pouted to himself, making a self-assured vow.

You gon' pay for having such a smart-ass mouth bitch. That I can promise.

Pissed, Charlotte stopped in the middle of the street, put the car in reverse, and made a U-turn, hopping on a nearby expressway, headed back towards Abercorn Street, where the probation office was located.

In this moment Charlotte made a promise to herself to bring press around more to eliminate any possible misunderstandings or sexual advances. Preston Mcgurt was the man that stole her heart five years ago and she wasn't willing to jeopardize her future with him for anyone. With this in mind, Charlotte made a silent pack with herself as well.

Who in the hell does Mr. Hill think he is? Press? No, he's definitely not my man. Not even close. And how could he take one conversation during lunch as a flirtatious jester? Starting tomorrow. I'm bringing my mase

Picking up his cell phone, press dialed grandma Mcgurt's phone #. He hadn't spoken to her in a while and he needed to hear the comfort of her voice.

"Hey grandma. How you?" He asked, once the line was connected.

"Tired chile, tired. I been cooking and cleaning all day," Grandma Mcgurt informed.

"I know I'll have me a plate ready. I'll be over there," Press promised.

They talked for a little while longer, mostly about his job. He told her that he had been at this particular one for six months now, and that he was enjoying it quite a bit. He also promised to bring Charlotte by to see her more often.

"You know Adam's coming home Friday. Tandra's planning on throwing him a welcome home party."

"That's good. I hope he stays out this time."

"Chile, me and u both. You think he's gonna be on roll ups?"

"You mean papers?"

"Yeah. Papers?"

"He should. Eve said that he received a split sentence, ten years, serve four. So more than likely he'll be on probation. Especially since he just about served all of his parol time in prison."

"O. Well. I just hope that his roll up person is as nice as that girl of yours."

"That's paper's grandma," Press huffed in frustration, correcting the much older woman again.

"Don't change the subject," Grandma hissed.

"Grandma. I know where your heading with this. And I don't like it."

"Is something wrong with you grandson? Are they putting crack inside of those doughnuts that you'all are eating? That's your cuzin boy. You better like it," Grandma Mcgurt threatened.

After ending the call, Press picked up the 48 laws of power book written by Robert green and he started to read. Over the years, Press and Adam barely spoke and their relationship was nowhere near as close as his and eve's. Although they were his first cousins alike eve was more like a sister to him whereas Adam was more like a distant relative.

Press thought about his Grandma. The old lady needed a vacation. Becuase she was a trip. Always had been. She wanted Charlotte to be Adam's probation officer. And she wasn't taking no for an answer.

◆ ◆ ◆

"Are you sure you heard what you said? Absolutely positive? Because that's one helluva accusation," Agent Love said from behind the driver's seat of a government sponsored vehicle. At this point Him and agent jones had been staking out this particular area for awhile.

"I'm more than sure. What else do you call telling ranger that he wants to be moved to another unit? I know what I heard," agent jones argued defensively.

"I'm telling you Love. That mufucka is probably the one that reported you to the internal affairs."

Agent Jones continued to publicly voice his concerns about Press being an informat for the internal affairs. Then Agent Love hopped out of the unmarked car they were driving in angrily. Jones's revealation was good. Yet disturbing.

For thirty minutes, Agent Love had been waiting on this particular guy to show up and finally his car had just pulled up into the driveway. As Agent Love approached the guy, he made a mental note to confront press later.

As soon as Agent Love approached the guy, he slapped him upside the head with the butt of the pistol. Three times.

"BAP! BAP! BAP!"

"You told on me? Hun mufucka?" Agent Love shouted, as he continued to pistol whip the man. Agent jones ran up behind him immediately after this took place.

"I don't know what you're talking about," the man pleaded. Then Agent Love slammed the guy's head on the back of his trunk repeatedly.

BAM! BAM! BAM!

"You reported me to the internal affairs?

BAM!

"Hun?"

BAM!

"HUN? Love repeated.

BAM!!!

"You thought I wasn't gonna find out didn't cha? *SNITCH!*" Love yelled, as he smashed the man's face against the car contiuously.

"LEAVE' DAT' MAN ALONE! HOW YOU GON' HATE SNITCHES' AND YOU THE POLICE!"

"FUCK OFF DAT MAN!!" Some random dude yelled from across the street.

Agent Love turned around and yelled back.

"MIND YO BUSINESS!" In response. Agent jones chipped in and started threatening the man as well.

"I BET YALL WON'T TRY ME LIKE THAT!!" Somebody else yelled.

"ME NEITHER!!!" The group of observers chirped in unison.

Seeing the crowd of angry witnesses grow, they left. After he exposed the alledged snitch with the wrath of humiliation, Agent Love hurried back to his car with haste.

"Bombaclot informer," Agent Love spoke, using his Jamaican accent.

◆ ◆ ◆

Later that night, Agent Love found himself walking out of a deserted looking building they referred to as their precinct. Located on Savannah's bull street, this was the designated spot for all the CNT agents. Captain Ranger had just pulled off not even five whole minutes before this. On this particular night, the two of them had been reviewing tomorrow's assignment-like usual. But for some reason, Agent Love wondered why Ranger hadn't mentioned that Press wanted to be transferred to another unit. Witholding information wasn't Rangers forte.

Imma have to start watching him too. Sneaky ass.

Nearing his sports car, Agent Love started to question his boss man's loyalty. He was starting to wonder if he could really trust him or not.

BLAT! BLAT! BLAT! BLAT! BLAT! BLAT!...BLAT!!!

All of a sudden multiple gun shots flew in Agent Love's direction. Soon, more followed, which ricochet off the precinct building thereby forcing a hole through his drop top convertible.

Ducking, Agent Love reached for his holster. He grabbed his own gun. But he was too late.

"NO, YOU MIND YO BUSINESS...PIGG!" The shooter yelled right before shoving the gear back into drive and speeding off.

Realizing that he took a bullet in the foot, Agent love inspected his bullet-holed car.

"Gonna cost me a fortune. Goddamit."

Love mumbled out loud, clearly pissed by the near-death experience and ridiculed car. Not only did he get hit, but he had no idea how to get revenge. It wasn't like he took the man's name down that he threatened earlier. Knowing that he would never find out who the shooter was, Agent Love did the only thing that he could do at the moment: *Nothing.*

And even though he'd never admit it, he was scared shitless, and thankful that he walked away with his life. After all. Minor damages to a vehicle was a lot better than death.

CHAPTER 12
No friendnemies

Adam's return was the talk of the town. Hundreds came out to party on his behalf. Friends, ex-girlfiends, and Hood celebrities alike were in the mix. Tandra was very popular in the urban community. So much so that she sent half the city invitations, hoping to make this event for her son both extravagant and memorable.

As promised, Tandra threw Adam a welcome home party. It was massive. Balloons were in abdunace, as well as paper-plates, cups, and hineken bottles. Free, endless food was supplied compliments of a local foodtruck and chef. The guest were given drinks of their choice. Patron and Ciroc were among the favorites. The aroma of maryjane was also in attendance, despite it being filled with off duty cops. The entire Mcgurt family was present, including the Chief of Police, the man responsible for the party's heavy police presence. He was the only uninvited guest.

"Adam. C'mere. Taste this," Tandra ordered from behind the grill. She gave a piece of meat a taste test before flipping it over onto the grill with a spatchler.

Adam sampled the meat while rubbing his belly.

Mmm

"Don't mmm me. I wanted you to sample *it*. *Not* my finger."

"My bad ma."

"Just don't let it happen again. Mike Tyson."

"Still got a sense of humor ma. U funnie."

"And so is your uncle. Why the hell are those cops here? O hell naw."

After a while, Adam convinced his mom to cease any potential confrontation between her and her brother for the sake of the reunion. Of course, she was hesitant, and reluctant. But if securing her son's love and approval meant postponing this beef, then that's what she intended on doing. For now.

Following this, the conversation continued.

"I saw you over there all booed-up. Mack daddy. Whats her name? Hepatites?" Tandra joked. She was Adam's mother, but their relationship, and bond, was more like brother and sister.

"You crazy ma."

"Crazy my ass. You kno how u do," Tandra laughed.

Just then Eve and Press walked up together.

"Why're yall getting quiet? Wat yall talkin' bout?" Eve asked out of curiosity.

"Nothin."

"O don't get smart ni. You went to jail and did 2-push-ups and now u think you tough. Big ass head," Eve teased.

They all talked for a while and reminisced on each other's childhood. Everyone except for Press and Adam. The two of them didn't have much to say to each other because they didn't have anything in common.

After the conversation subsided, Adam pulled his twin sister to the side. The two of them were now having a private conversation.

"I'm telling you sis. I'on trust dat' nigga."

"That's our cousin," Eve defended.

"And? That mufucka CNT. Fuck him. You said he threatened to lock you up rite? Aiight then. Family doesn't make idle threats. He's Five-fuckin-O sis. End of story."

"He was joking."

"Family don't joke like that. Fuck him," Adam repeated, disrespectfully.

Realizing that Adam's opinion about Press wouldn't change, Eve switched subjects. "I see uncle Press had you hemmed up? You know, for someone that doesn't like the police, you sure were just around plenty. Unc was surrounded by cops.

"See, that's different. Do you realize that our uncle is the most powerful person in the city? I mean. He's the fuckin Chief for god sake. Huge difference."

"So what do you think about Charlotte?"

"Who. Robocop's girl? She aiight. Not my type. Fine, but messy. That bitch ask me like million questions."

"She's the police bro what did you expect."

"Figures."

"O you didn't kno? My bad, Eve grinned. She's not that bad. Matterfact, she's suppose to be helping you find a job."

"In law-enforcement?"

"You wish. Just go talk to the lady Monday morning, bighead. Aiight?"

"Aiight."

After thinking this over, Adam was confused. Eve had her back turn already walking off at this point. "Why our cousin just can't get me one? His police ass. O, I get it. He doesn't want to be bothered with me. That's cool. The feeling is mutual. I like his girl better anywayz."

"Thought she wasn't your type."

"I lied."

"Good. Now run and tell her the good news. She's *your* probation officer," Eve informed devilishly.

◆ ◆ ◆

Two weeks passed by in no time since the day that Adam was released from prison. And to Press's surprise, he was doing the right thing for once. Charlotte reported good things about Adam. But this was unusual for one of her paroles. In fact, the two of them had unexpectedly formed a bond that was quite impressive, considering the circumstances. On the other hand, Press knew that his girl could be a bitch at times. She was always professional. Always. So that meant that if Adam slipped up even once, she'd violate his supervised release on probation, cousin in law or not. This is the reason why press hated the idea of charlotte becoming adam's PO in the first place because he knew that it would all come back to haunt him eventually.

CNT Agent Mcgurt hopped out of the unmark car as it came to a hault. Today was just another day on the job and they were doing what they did on a regular basis: Jumping out on dope boys.

Immediately dudes took off running. The trap went from a place of business to a race track within seconds. One of the dudes tried to hop a fence but he got stuck thanks to his sagging pants, which were already too big, and the reason he was caught..

"C'mere," Agent jones managed in between breathing heavy.

"Slow bastard. I smoke too much to let you outrun me."

The other agents came shortly. Apparently, most of the trap's hustlers out ran the counter narcotic's agents. Even press, and he didn't even smoke.

They all huddled around as agent jones searched the man's personnel. Today was Agent Love's first day back. After having surgery, he was released from memorial's hospital. But the bullet wound was fresh and still weeks away from healing so he had to walk using a crutch for leg support.

"You mean to tell me dat' yall didn't catch any of those those little shits. Somebody better give me some answers," Agent Love demanded angrily after witnessing everything transpire. Upon the completion of his investsigation, and brief rant, Agent love punched-out the car window in a heated rage.

The narcs escorted the two non-running hustlers to a nearby patty-wagon with handcuffs. Press remained calmed and observant.

"Mcgurt. Search him. Right now," Agent Love demanded, pointing to one of the slow dope boys. There was a full crowd of citizens on the block. On the very next street everyone and their mom was out. They were having a block party.

Shocked, press informed Love that the guy had been searched.

"So. Wat's' dat suppose to mean? And hurry the fuck up."

Press, barely keeping his composure, thought about Agent Love's comment. He figured that his mood swing was due to him being shot so press did as he was told and decided not to be combative. Making the man spread his legs, narc-agent Mcgurt searched the guys pockets. This didn't go without a hassle. Apparantly, the dope boy was pissed, cursing and shouting like a lunatic.

"Get the fuck off of me! U stank breath having, dick in the booty ass PIG! Imma drag you, Rupaul," the guy intimidated.

"*Love.* All you gotta do is loosin theses cuffs. Bet I beat' his ass."

After coming up short, Press looked and saw a small tattoo written on the side of the guy's hand. It read in big bold letters. "EAT ME."

"Found anything?"

Press shook his head at Love's question.

"But you didn't search *everywhere* now did chu?"

Embarrassed, Press rolled his eyes at agent jones, who had made the last comment. Repositioning himself to pat the assaliant down, again, he held his breath as the foul mouth man slaughtered him verbally. Press was called everything but a child of god. And although they were meaningless words, they were starting to agitate him.

After the second search, Press found two ounces of crack cocaine, embodied in a zip lock bag. Shortly thereafter Mr. Eat me was placed inside of A patty wagon. But this was irrelevant during the drive to the jailhouse. Press was given specifc instructions to become the guy's temporary excort. However, the presence of a law enforment vehicle wouldn't prevent the disrespect and high profanity usage. Press was responsible for taking the guy to jail alone so his eardrums were filled with hostil language and terroristic threats.

And all it took was for him to degrade himself. Sacrifice produced promotions, and promotions was the sole purpose of press's journey. Sacrifice was not just a method, it was a task, a task that wasn't always easy, and occasionally embarrassing.

Especially when it consisted of searching a grownmans butthole for drugs in the presence of hundreds of eye witnesses.

Later that day, after stopping by a local gas station, Agent Love made a U-turn, heading towards West Savanah's Fell-wood Holmes. Absent his crutch, he was on his way to speak to one of his master-splinter's. After three weeks of suffering, finally his doctor decided to remove his crutch and this had him in a better mood.

Thinking about Press, Agent Love remembered how he embarrassed him. That was weeks ago. They were cool now. Why couldn't Press just understand that they were on the same team? Okay, sure, he gave away dope to snitches, pocketed a little drug money, and smoked a lil bit of weed, big deal. Didn't make him a bad person. In Agent Love's eyes these things weren't crimes. They were law's written by the white man, formulated to minimize the growth of black entrepreneurs. Alcohol and Cigarettes killed people all the same and yet they legalized that, why? Because it could be taxed, that's why. Certain laws Agent Love just didn't agree with so he'd make'em, brake' em, and enforce' em, *if* he chose too. Sure, there are dope boys that deserve to be in prison. But for the most part, trap boys was just trying to feed their families like everyone else. Wasn't like the drug dealers were out raping women or molesting children. Now those were the creeps that deserved to be locked away as far as Agent Love was concerned.

Cops and criminals are supposed to be enemies, but in many ways they reflect one another. The dealers who deserved to be punished was the kingpin's and drug lords that forgot about their communities once they were successful. If you made it big on the behalf of the people in your community, regardless, if they were crack-heads or not, you should give back. Was that notion too much to ask? If so, those trappers deserved exactly what was coming to them: *Love's wrath.*

Press couldn't sympathize with love's approach. Why not? The event that took place was put in place to show Press who was boss. As far as Agent Love was concerned Press could transfer to another unit if he chose to do so it wouldn't cramp his style one bit. Love became bothered once he heard that press was a possible informat. This news was devastating. And jeopardized the integrity of his organization. That's when the lines were blurred. Didn't matter how much of a good cop he thought Press was. Whenever Press did depart it'd be cool. But as long as he remained he had to lose the ego and follow orders. Theses conditions were non negotiable and required to those under the direct influence of Love's leadership.

CHAPTER 13

911 is a joke

"So. How's Matt? He's not acting up is he? That boy stayed in trouble in school, Charlotte said as she laid her head on Press's lap. I still can't believe that he's a cop. It just doesn't seem like his thing."

Noticing the lack of communication from her significant other, she slapped him on the top of his forehead playfully. "Why are you ignoring me? I know you heard me."

"Sorry bae. I was in a zone."

"Matt's ok. I guess. Heard you dated his cousin." Press turned the conversation around now playing the victim. He wasn't interested in discussing work so he just pretending to listen. Soon he resumed his train of thought as Charlotte tried to explain.

Today marked one year since the day that press decided to join the counter narcotics taskforce unit. Initially, the environment had him on pens and needles. However, eventually, he got into the groove of things and just ran with the flow. Press learned to compromise. If his colleague's chose to go outside of the guideline's to catch criminals that didn't concern him. His job description required arresting drug dealers the old fashion way: *by the book.*

Two months ago he asked the captain to put him in for a transfer to another unit. Not that he couldn't handle the heat, he wasn't the one in the kitchen. Actually, press would never admit it, but he became fascinated with the narcs. They demanded respect. And even tho he didn't agree with the tactics, they meant business and were a effective team. Drug dealers almost shitted themselves whenever they showed up and it felt good to be apart of such a highly feared organization.

But press and Charlotte relocated to the Garden City area, just on the outskirts of the inner city, a few months ago. The drive to work was starting to weigh its load. The bull street precinct and his home was on the opposite parts of town nearly a forty minute commute.

Captain Ranger promised press that after six more months with them, and a clean behavior conduct report, he'd honor his request. The minimum amount of time that was required at any given division before transferring to another department was eighteen months. So this meant that he only had six more months with this particular sector.

Press was upset about what transpired weeks ago. He was embarrassed at the expense of Agent love. This form of disrespect was only tolerated because he wanted to impress Ranger by fufilling the good conduct agreement.

Thinking back on his girl's question, press shook his head, mumbling to himself. For some reason unknown, work was starting to take a toll on his mental, and his feelings were detrimental in maintaining stability within him and Charlotte's relationship.

"Imma catch a charge next time. They're going to have to write me up for more than insubordination. Then Matt, love, or whatever is name is can kiss my ass. Six months .... I can behave' til then."

◆ ◆ ◆

The next day at work was an abnormal one. Agent Love called in sick. But he was the leader. So Agent Jones would be the acting superior until Agent Love's return.

As usual they cruised the streets of the *Seaport* in unmark cars. After six whole hours of doing the norm, they stopped by a local Chinese food restaurant for something to eat. Another narc, Agent Anderson, was the only agent who went inside to place their orders. He and Press had rode together in a separate vehicle.

"Yall see that?" Narc Jones pointed.

"What?" A back seated narcotics agent asked.

"Dat?" Narc Jones pointed again.

"That's Sabastian's car," another agent informed.

"Who?"

"Sabastian. Philo's nephew. You know. The kingpin. The prince. The mothafucka that sells meth. He run's the whole west side. I heard that he's suppose to be affiliated with this secret society of organized crime called the *UAT* (us against them). I even heard that they're like the mob for black people," the gossiping narc explained.

"I' on believe in fairytales."

"I don't care if his uncle's the president. I know one thing. That mustang's clean af," the backseater admired, wishing that he were Sabastian.

"What does af mean?"

"Don't you be on facebook? Dummie. As fuck."

"You ass fuck. I strictly pussy."

"Ok Chinese man."

"So what's the plan boss?" the other narc switched subjects in an attempt to avoid confrontation. The backseater wasn't all that bright in the brains department. And even dumber when it came to social media.

"Give me a minute," Agent Jones replied, as he hopped out of the car, heading towards the car that Press was in. Most of the time when they rode, they rode two, three, four, and even five cars deep. But Press never rode with agent jones during their drug raids.

What does he want now? That's why I don't rode with him. I don't want to be bothered. Plus he's an asshole."

"That's philo's newphew car right there," Narc Jones pointed to a green mustang that sat right across the street next to a furniture store.

"Yall follow us. Slowly. And don't get out the car until I say so. Gentlemen. We have ourselve's' a mark."

◆ ◆ ◆

Press didn't have a real problem with agent jones. He just didn't appreciate the way that he paraded his authority around. Jones was second in command and he went out of his way to let it be known. Jones always had a point to prove. He wanted the credit for arresting Philo's nephew. That's why they were pursuing sabastian. Not because he was currently committing a crime, like other suspects, they encounered during missions. Jones wanted to bring Sabastian down because he was envious. Point blank.

Agent Love always preplanned their assignments. Freestyling and reacting off of hunches wasn't something he did. Press had to applaud Agent Love for his success, even tho they could never quite get along. Agent Love went by word of mouth, a snitches information, and evidence that was more substantial and concrete. Unlike his right-hand man, love's assignments were premeditated and not linked to theories. `

After trailing Sabastian for blocks, the narcs forced him to pull over. They received a tip from an unknown source that he was dealing methamphetamine. He also had 2 kilos stashed in a secret stash spot. That's what agent jones explained to the other narc agent's. But Press wasn't as gullible.

The narcs searched Sabastian's car thoroughly. They searched his vehicle, trunk, socks, and derriere. They also searched his shoes, ashtrays, seats, glove department, and whatever else was visible. They even searched the little boy that he had with him right before searching the hat that he had on top of his head. Press could tell that the kid wasn't no more than eight or nine years old. That was probably sabastian's son Press figured. They did look alike.

Sabastian figured that he should've followed his intuition instead of letting his baby mom's talk him into buying a recliner as a present for his mom's birthday.

Originally, he planned to give his mom a shit load of money like he always did. But his child's mom convinced him otherwise. He thought about the crooked narc agents and the bogus anonymous tip they *allegedly* received about him trafficking methamphetamine. That was BS. Sure, he sold dope. But not meth. There was a big difference. Anybodie who was somebody knew his choice of drugs: loud, (high-grade marijuana), powder, and heroin.

Once his uncle heard about this, there would be consequences for the harassment, that much he knew. Sure, things were hilarious now but the real joke would be on them.

And to make matters worse, he had his daughter with him, Philo's great niece.

Good thing I just got rid of that last brick before stopping to the furniture store. Otherwise... I'd be fucked

The drug task-force agents continued to search Sabastian's personnel. At this point they were lingering outside of his car praying that they found some dope. Disregarding his kid, they continued the race to find the base. Nearly an hour had passed by already so quiting wasn't likely to happen any time soon.

Then all of a sudden narcotic agent jones came running towards sebastian's car like a bat out of hell. He had a plastic bag full of cocaine in his right hand.

"I found it. You almost had us. Not to worry. You' goindown sebastian."

"Cheer-up. I thought you liked your new bracelets," Narc Agent Jones antagonized. He read sebastian his miranda rights and pulled out a fresh set of cuffs.

Sebasian shook his head.

"Agent jones. You know that's not mine man, fo real."

"Whose is it?"

"Yours. I saw you pull it out your pants."

"Look. As you probably already know, I'm a very important person. So take off the cuffs. And maybe. Just maybe, you can keep your pathetic life."

"You'd do dat for little ol me? Thanks. Since we both in such giving moods I'll give you one, *second,* to shut the fuck up. Now be a good boy and call your uncle. Make sure you tell him he's next."

CHAPTER 14

Family fued

P acing her living room back and forth, Tandra inhaled the Newport cigarette smoke and blew it out slow. The conversation that she was having was working her last nerve.

"Bitch, are you crazie? Some niggaz just shot at your boyfriend's house and you around here worrying about what I cooked. Eve. I can't with you."

"I aint ate all day Ma."

"Is this a joke? Please tell me it is."

"Relax. Wasn't nobody even home. Lawd."

"So they wasn't looking for your boyfriend? The one that's out here robbing everybody'? I got ears."

"Stop' believing what' you hear ma. There rumors."

"I want you in this house before night-fall."

"But ma. Ughhhh. You get on my nerves. I aint coming nowhere. I'm grown."

"O you coming. Don't make me come over there and dragg you."

But ma y-

"Bring yo ass in this FUCKIN HOUSE EVE! NOW!!!" Tandra demanded, slamming the phone down aggressively.

Tandra stormed into her bedroom where her crack pipe was located. Then she placed a ten-dollar hit on the tip of her stem. Tandra wasn't a full fledged crack head. This was just something that she did occasionally, when tough moments like this occurred. Nobody else knew about her addiction. At least in her mind.

Finally calming down, Tandra sat down and started daydreaming. What was Eve's problem? The girl just didn't get it. First, she was with some guy named Tod, and now, she was dealing with a stick up kid/jack boy known as Polo. Time and time again Tandra tried to talk some sense into her only daughter. But eve wouldn't listen. Why did her twins grow up to be so terrible? Deep down, tandra knew the answer. She was the blame. Tandra never knew who her baby father was. So her family was practically the only relatives that her kids knew. She could only imagine how hard it must've effected them growing up without a dad. Helpessly, with a one-day mom. One day mom was here, the next day mom was in prison.

Tandra felt that her lack of guardianship and presence effected the way that her churn behaved. As kids, they suffered from the lack of attention. So now, as adults, they craved it.

Charlotte's office was located on Abercorn Street. This was her sanctuary and also the very place where she conducted supervised release interviews.

The office space was occupied with two chairs, one of which was designed for the housing official as well as the parolee. There was a lap-top that sat on top of a wooden table. Joint pictures of press and charlotte occupied the walls.

"Are you still at target's warehouse?" Charlotte interrogated from behind the seat where her lap-top sat.

"Mmm-hmm," the female probationer confirmed.

"You mighty quiet today aint cha?"

"Lot on my mind."

"I understand. So often, the mind tends to wonder. But Remain focus, no mater what. I know it's hard, especially working in a male dominated field. So much testosrone. As women: we have to stick together."

"Enough girl talk. Besides, I sense that your not interested in talking. So let's get your urine sample, so I can let you get back to those vigilant thoughts of yours."

Just then Press walked in with a slew of roses. Charlotte was about to take a lunch break and he wanted to surprise her.

"Sup," Press greeted the girl. He didn't know where he knew the girl from, but she looked familiar. He couldn't quite put his finger on it, and he sure wasn't about to ask in front of his girl, especially since she was the girl's probation officer.

She's a dime. And I'm not talkin silver coins. What's a' fine tenderony like dat' doin' on probation?

After the female probationer's urine sample was collected, and press departed with his adultress thoughts, the young, fine, specimen strutted down the hallway. All the eyes were on her.

The lightskin beauty tooted her nose in response to the test results.

"This bitch keeps trying to catch me slippin. I'on even smoke."

Charlotte, aka Mrs. Blink, the god fearing PO, was considered a bitch amongst her probationer's. Even her colleagues hated her guts, especially Pat, who once praised the hollow ground that she walked on. Mrs. Blink was rumored to have sent hundreds, if not thousands of people back to prison for violationg probation. Jailhouse was Charlotte's middle name. She had a fascination for revocation.

Mrs. Stink. Can't stan' dat hoe. Uglie ass. But her man. Ni he can geit. With a capitol G. Wonder what he sees in her?

CHAPTER 15

Yay or nay

Slamming the cabinet, Eve stormed out the kitchen headed towards the bathroom in a frustrated manner.

It aint neva nothing to eat here. Freekin hate dis place.

Eve was disgusted with the living conditions. Not even a full two years ago, she purchased the home for her mom and already it looked like a disaster, as if the place had been desimated by a tsunami.

Eve understood her mom's concern. But she could handle her own affairs. Besides, the thug that shot at her mother-in-laws house was't a threat. (Her boyfriend lived with his mom) They were just a few sucker's that her roughneck boyfriend polo' roughed up. The shots, however, were for show. Entertainment. If one of those bullets were to hit her *flesh,* world war three would soon follow, thanx to her no job having, psychotic, sinificant other.

Exiting the bathroom, Eve thought about her own reputation and how her character was always in question. Eve was wrongfully stereotyped. Everybody always made her out to be the bad guy. But she wasn't. She was a bad bitch, and there was a significant difference. Sure, in the past, she set dudes up to get robbed. She even took stuff from them with no help. In Eve's mind, she was justified, because she only took from those that deserved it. She only robbed, or co-robbed, baller's that weren't genuine. Men that threw money in clubs for no reason were on her shitlist. Those that neglected their responsibilities as fathers were top candidates. This rattled her anger every time she saw a baller throw away chips, because in some cases, their offspring, was out begging for some.

There was only one guy that Eve regretted robbing. It was her ex, during her stay in Charleston South Carolina. The couple remained the center of attention and often fought amongst one another mostly about his adulterous affairs. One night, after a heated argument turned fist fight, she was left with two black eyes and a busted lip. The results which emerged after she confronted him about some big booty stripper that he was reportedly sleeping with. The confrontation followed shortly thereafter. Eve pretended like she was calling the police on him just to get him to leave. When he did, so did she, with all of his shit, including the money that he often bragged so much about. Eve took it all. Then she relocated back home, to Savannah, where she started spending *his* money like it grew on trees. She bought her mom that house, put money inside of her brother Adam's prison account, and she opened up a day care with the rest of the geechie boy's money.

Tod was another one of Eve's ex's. The two had grew up together. Because of that factor she entrusted him with a large portion of Carolina boy's product. Eve, acting as tod's girl, and sponsor, was the single-handed reason for tod's success. She took a dope charge for him. Tod was relieved. Eve never served any time despite entering into a guilty plea. She got Probation.

Things went left when she received a call from a girl claiming to be pregnant with tod's baby. Which lead to the home invasion, strategized and organized by her, tandra's daughter, *Eve*, Seaport's diva and heartbroken drama queen.

Today, both of Eve's ex's were history, including her daycare. Gullibly, she let tod's sister manage it, which proved to be a bad idea, and ultimately, a bad investment. The couple's departure encouraged a very profound laziness, namely on the behalf of her brother loving sister-in-law.

Eve blew all Carolina boy's money. That's when she met polo.

He was both the man of her dreams and nightmares. He was extremely jealous, but yet, unexpectingly kind. Dumb as a box of rocks, but smart as a whistle. Heaven sent, but crazy as hell.

Eve thought about Tandra, her mom. Did she really think that no one knew about her drug habit? The news spreaded like a wildfire, everyone knew, because tandra was too obvious, and oblivious. Smoking weed was one thing. But unexplained absences, and crack-pipes were another.

Hanging up her iPhone, Eve felt a sense of relief. She thought about her mom again. Deep down inside, she knew that her mom only wanted the best for her. But staying in one spot wasn't her thing. Eve was always on a mission. But now, she was in hibernation. For now. This would all change once Polo arrived.

Stepping out of her office into the lobby, Charlotte spotted one of her probationers. He was sitting down inside of the lobby waiting on her to summon him inside her office. He was reading one of those *hip hop weekly magazines.*

After calling him to the back, they headed towards her office. The whole time they were walking the guys mind was racing. His thoughts were cautious.

I hope she don't accuse me of smelling' like weed' again. Maybe I shouldn't've just smoked that joint.

"Ms. Blink. I aint kno' Charlotte was your real name. Sexy. I know yo' parents had that nursey-rhymes in mind when they named you. Charotte's web."

"I'd love to be caught in yo' web charlotte."

"Mr. Tanis. You think supervised release is a joke don't you?" Charlotte blurted. Tanis's flirtatious jester was rejected.

"Of course not. Why would you think that? I'm sorry. Pardon

me for complimenting a beautiful woman, which is against the law."

"Keep the sarcasm Mr. Tanis you know that's not what I'm talking about."

"Then what are you talking about Ms. Blinks? I hope it's not because no-one wants to hire me? Come on now. Convicted felons finish last."

"Mr. Tanis. I personally talked to the manager at Burger King and gave you an opportunity since you seem to be having such a hard time finding employment."

"You rite. But when I went down there to fill out an application, he wasn't there," Tanis said lying through his teeth. He wasn't a fast-food job having mothafucka.

"Well I don't think you're trying hard enough Mr. Tanis. First of all, you were home for almost three months now and you haven't secured any gainful employment. And second, you haven't made any payments towards your fine," Charlotte threatened, letting the severity of his action's sink in.

"I think you need a vacation. Maybe then you'll be more assertive."

"Ms. Blinks I'm trying, I swear to god. You know I got two kids & I'm on child support. I got 2 two dollar hoe's for babymothers. Please don't take me away from my kids again. Please, that's all I ask. Three weeks. Imma have a job I promise. Just give me three weeks. And Imma make a payment too. Matterfact, what time yall close? He asked, fronting like hell. Tanis knew all to well what time the probation office closed. What person on papers didn't?

"Please Ms. Blinks, pretty please. Have a heart," Tanis begged.

"Mr. Tanis ... I don't know ... Something just tells me that you're not going to do the right thing," Charlotte said thinking about his two kids remark. It was the oldest excuse in the book. Everyone and their mother used that line. Literally.

He's kinda right. Felons do have it rough. Maybe I am being unreasonable.

"One week. Its all you have. Make it count."

Relieved, Tanis thanked her and proceeded to leave.

She could've gave me another three weeks. Gonna' have to get a job for real this time. No bullshit.

"Mr. Tanis!" Charlotte yelled, chasing him down before he exited the building without her consent. He had already made it to his car by now.

"I need a urine sample. I'm sorry. I forgot."

"You didn't smell like marijuana today. I'm so proud of you Mr. Tanis."

"Now follow me. You know the procedure."

Two months passed since the day that Sebastian was arrested. He was out on bond awaiting trial now and the chances of him being convicted were very slim.

Agent Jones and the other three narcotic's agents that was in the car that day were fired not even three weeks after sabastian's arrest. Captain Ranger wasn't sure how all of this happened. The only thing that he knew for sure was that his superior called him demanding the termination. Allegedly, Philo had the mayor in his pocket.

Agent Anderson was set to testify. But one witness wasn't enough to convince the jury of Sabastian's guilt. So from the looks of things Philo's family was about to make the judicial system look like fucking idiots.

After explaining the above paragraph to Press, Captain Ranger poured himself a cup of coffee like he always did around this time. Then. He started sipping. Real slow.

"So. Mcgurt. You were on the scene. What did you see?"

"I saw jones. He picked it up."

"So sabastian didn't throw the dope?"

"Probably did. I dunno. But I didn't see it. *Personally.*"

Captain Ranger nodded his head disappointingly. And sipped his coffee some more. Much slower than he did earlier. Press was always an interesting guy he thought. Press was honorable. And noble.

"Mcgurt. How many more months do you have with us?"

"Four."

"That soon?"

Press never replied. He just stared.

"I did say that I'd recommend you for a transfer didn't I?"

Following a moment of silence, Captain Ranger continued. "You know Mcgurt. There's this story about the inmate and the warden. Ever hear of it?"

Press shook his head.

"Well. Let me tell you all about it son," Captain Ranger said, placing his hands on the back of his head. Then he propped his feet up on the top of his desk.

"There was once this inmate named Mike. Mike served most of his prison sentence, having only two years left, in which he wanted to relocate to a halfway house to serve the remainder. He stepped to the warden, asked for assistance, and the warden agreed, promising him a free trip to the justice department's safe haven."

"Two weeks later, he found out that his mistress was having an affair, the same one he hired just months prior as a correctional officer."

"This time, the warden stepped to Mike, asking him to stab the inmate, assuring him that he'd be protected if the department of justice decided to get involved. But Mike refused," Captain Ranger informed, looking Press square in his eyes.

"Take a wild guess what happened?"

"Mike never made it to the halfway house".

"So you are familiar with this story? *Dirty dog,*" Captain Ranger blushed, revealing an old wrinkle face and damaged teeth.

They talked a little while longer before Press got up to leave. On his way out the door, Press thought about what had just transpired between him and his superior. No, he'd never heard the story. But decoding encrypted languages was his specialty. The message was pricise. And clear. If press went into that courtroom during trial and said anything that would compromise the integrity of the law enforcement community, the only transfer that he'd be making is the one that relates to unemployment.

CHAPTER 16

"Don't do it press"

In no time three full months passed since the day that Press was asked to testify against sabastian. Today was the day before trial. It was almost time to show and prove. But Press was still indecisive. He wasn't sure what he'd do. The stakes were twice as high for him because any betrayal on his end would invite consequences.

Press was one hundred percent sure that agent jones planted the dope on sabastian that day. Every fiber in his bones stated the obvious. The arrest and probable cause was frivolous. What transpired was wrong and no justification would suffice and stand up in a court of law.

Laying her head on press's lap, charlotte stared into his eyes. They already had this disscussion a million times but charlotte was extremely adamant about getting through to him.

"Just tell the truth bae. You can always get another job. Screw Ranger."

Taking her advice into consideration, Press just remained silent. He didn't really want to talk about it. Yet he had a burning desire to hear her opinion.

"Now I've been staying out of the madness that goes on at your job long enough. Only because I always knew, deep down, that you'd make the right decisions. But now. I'm not so sure," Charlotte confessed.

"All citizens deserve equal protection. Even those on the opposite side of the law. Look at me bae, I'm serious, Charlotte demanded, turning press's face towards hers. I get that you're confused. I really do. But you don't need that sort of thing lingering on your conscience. We'll stay if we have to and put transferring on hold."

"Doing your job is one thing. But sending an innocent man to prison, regardless of how much drugs he's presumed to sell, is wrong press and I won't forgive you if you decide to go thru with it, I'm sorry. You don't have to be a saint. But I be dam if you become the devil."

On the way to his Dad's office, Press went into deep thought. He just came from visiting his mom and her advice resembled his girl's, which wasn't surprising. His mother was a truthful person and she raised him to have honest morals.

Press could almost predict what kind of advice his dad would give. After all, Sabasian was Philo's nephew, and his dad, the Chief of Police, had formed an inseparable bond with Philo ever since that day his life was spared nearly seventeen years ago. As a kid, Press must've heard that story a million times. And even tho Philo was allegedly apart of one of the biggest criminal organizations that America had ever seen, he was still the Chief's friend, and real friends didn't abandon one another, regardless of career choices. These were just some of the principles that Press was raised on so he was one hundred percent sure about his predictions regarding his dad's advice.

Within minutes Press arrived at his Dad's office. The secretary made a call, told the Chief who was present, and just like that, Press was summoned into the massive office.

"Mr. big shot. Finally made time to come see his old man. I'm appalled," The Chief teased.

"Don't be. I came to borrow some money," Press joked, right before taking a seat. Curiously, he stared at a picture of black jesus that was nailed to the cross.

"Cute. But your fishing in the wrong pond son. I'm so broke I can barely pay attention."

"Sabasian's lawyer call you?" Press blurted, addressing the true reason why he was there.

The Chief nodded his head. "Said you told him that you'd testify on the States behalf. But you didn't seem like you wanted too."

Why is Sabastian's attorney calling my father if I already spoke to him? Something's not adding up. I'm making a mental note right now to investigate this later.

"So what should I do pops?"

"What the hell do you mean what should you do?" The Chief replied in disbelief.

"You didn't see him throw any drugs did you?"

Press shook his head.

"Well that's what you say in court. Don't be a hypocrite. We raised you better than that preston."

After letting these words marinate, the Chief of police started shaking his head disappointingly. "I told you that this would happen didn't I? Didn't I tell you what you were getting yourself into? But no, you were just too stubborn."

Annoyed, the chief of police chose his words very carefully before he spoke again.

"I think you forget sometimes just how much influence I have around here. If you're afraid of what someone thinks, namely your boss, don't be. *I'm* the boss of all bosses here in chatham coutny."

CHAPTER 17

Subscriction to a free trial

T oday was the day of trial. Reporters from all over the southeastern part of Georgia competed for an opportunity to interview Eugene Shabazz, also known as sabastian. But sabastian and his attorney had no comments for the media. They both dodged questions and wanted to brag after they were victorious.

The courtroom was packed to its mass capacity. Almost every resident in the entire city came out to witness the judge's verdict. Sabastian was infamous for destroying families through the crack epidemic so supporting his demise justified such a massive attendance.

Ortega was sabastian's lawyer. He a trial champion. His resume extended throughout the entire state of Georgia. Whenever Attorney Ortega decide to take a case, lots of fame was gained, and very few victories went unclaimed. Ortega was a dope boys dream. But his growing reputation continued to expand his popularity, which was bad news for petty hustlers. If one of his potential clients wasn't talking about spending big cash, the retainment would fail, like a student turned stripper who neglected her studies.

Folding his arms, and tapping his gator shoes against the floor, Ortega cleared his throat.

"I'm telling you Eugene. If one of those agents get on that stand and say that they saw you throw anything, anything at all, you're going to prison, for a long, long time. Your family maybe powerful but the word of someone in law enforcement is like an iron clad prenup, solid. A potential clash with an officer that lie's is inevitable because they tend to stick together. Whenever this occurs a conviction usually follows," Attorney Ortgea informed shrugging his shoulders.

He waited for a couple of seconds before regaining his speech. "I think you should consider taking the plea offer eugene. Before it's too late," Ortega advised.

"Let me get this straight. You want me, an innocent-man, quote on quote, to confess to something that I didn't even do? You fuckin lawyers are Idiots."

"Eugene. Those are fuckin narcs. One testimony is all it takes to convince a jury," Ortega explained.

"Hey fuck face. You're my fuckin lawyer in case you forgot. Who's side are you on? The district attonerys?"

"But Eu-

"Are you deaf? Because I don't see a hearing-aid back there. You don't speak English mufucka. Gracias por nada ese. Senor Punta."

"Now run' and' tell dat cum-swallowin bitch nancy to take dat plea and go fuck herself."

Meanwhile, Nancy Collins was doing some prepping of her own. Known for her determination, quick wit, and grimmey tactics, she was infamously known to persuade the accused into taking shady plea offers. Nancy was the leading district attorney for the southeastern region of Georgia. Unlike Attorney Ortega, her track record wasn't as impressive when it came to trial. Tho Nancy claimed a few victories, she lost way more than she won.

But the infamous Philo's case was different. Philo was at the top of the list as far as criminal prosecution. If Nancy managed to convict his nephew this would satisfy both the community and but her own ego. Counselman Ortega had been winning high profile cases for decades. But today, Nancy had a feeling that this would all come to an end. This battle meant everything to her and she'd do everything in her power to make her prediction a reality.

Nancy continued to prepare the states witnesses for trial. Although the trial itself would take a couple of days, the most crucial part's depended on Today's testimonies.

After going over everything and rehearsing what she wanted the narc agents to say on the stand, Nancy, the leading district attorney, asked them individually if they had any questions. Press did. His questions were confrontational.

"I do," Press announced, as he pulled Nancy to the side to chat in private.

Shortly after getting her undivided attention, Press held the back of his head in a state of confusion. "Look Nancy. I didn't see Eugene throw anything."

"And?"

"And that's a innocent man nancy. I'm not feeling it."

"Agent Mcgurt. This happens all the time. Some officers feel like they have to do everything by the book. Which is how it should be don't get me wrong. But some measures can be justified in light of the circumstances. Deep down inside you know he's guilty. That motherfucker sells more drugs than the doctors prescribe. The whole city knows about Philo and his family tree of terrorists."

"I mean, c'mon Mcgurt. Ok. Maybe he didn't commit this specific crime. But you're acting like he deserves a Nobel peace prize. Jeez. Trap boys, or whatever it is that they're calling themselves these days, don't deserve metals. Unless it's the kind that goes around their wrists."

"You sure think highly of him considering the circumstances. You're a cop in case you forgot. People like us don't intermingle with crooks. Is he paying you off?," Nancy accused, more as an accusation than a question. But after noticing the offended look on Press's face, she breathed a sigh of relief.

"If he beats us, he'll be pushing that poison to these kids the minute he leaves this courtroom."

Seeing that her words was affecting Press's reasoning, Nancy kept preaching.

"The judicial system was made to enforce justice, not be made a mockery of. Criminals are animals that know how to manipulate the law. So we have to use tactics that may not always seem right, but in the end, are necessary," Nancy convinced, praying that Press would come to his senses. She refused to back down just because his conscience was overtaking his manhood.

"Whatever you decide to do just know that you can't back out now because I subpoenaed you as a witness for the state. So you have one of two choices. You can do what's best for the community, and send him to prison. Or you can put him back on the streets so he can poison our babies," Nancy preached, narrowing down Press's ultimatum.

"The choice is yours," she reiterated.

Nancy's speech was so dramatic and convincing that you would've thought that she was campaigning for president. She was almost confident that she had gotten through to him. But after closer inspection, she withdrew these feelings. Nancy was no mind reader, and the blank expression on Press's face couldn't assist her either. At this point she wasn't sure what he'd do.

On the way to the courtroom, Nancy picked up a full bottle of Ibuprofen. Because she was definitely about to be sick if Press got on that stand and did the unthinkable.

◆ ◆ ◆

The trial began within minutes. Nancy decided to let Agent

Anderson testify first, that way Press would have a really simple blueprint and story to corroborate, which would lessen the burden on him and be a source of guidance.

After Ortega was done cross examining Agent Anderson, Nancy called Press to the stand. She began with the basics asking him to state his name, occupation, job description, and location on the day of the alleged crime. She asked him if he recognized the defendant and he nodded his head. Then she asked Press to recount that day and explain it to the court.

Press's revelation was identical to narcotic agent Anderson's. But for some reason he was hesitating to say exactly what it was that he observed and this was starting to scare the living shit out of Nancy.

"So-- "*Agent Mcgurt*," Nancy paused, tired of beating around the bush. She started sucking her teeth and rolling her eyes. "Did you see the defendant, she pointed, Eugene Shabazz, otherwise known as Sabastian, throw any drugs on the ground?"

"*No*," Press confessed, shocking the court. This revelation was huge to the jury and court alike because normally the state's witness is summoned to help the prosecution not the defense attorney.

Sabastian smiled abroad as he fumbled with his thoughts.

I knew the Chief wouldn't let me and unc down. He said he'd talk with his son. And talk he did. Good lookin' out. I Gotta brake bread. Fuck face don't get shit

"No further questions your honor," Nancy said in defeat, not bothering to call another witness. The case was over she reasoned. Special Agent Mcgurt made a complete fool out of her.

"Court adjorned? I wasn't finish."

"Sure you weren't. But you'll be once I report your testimony to your boss. Heard you told him different.

"Congratulations Mcgurt," Nancy said giving him a round of

applause ungenuniely. She was pissed.

"You did a good job making a fool out of the ENTIRE STATE OF GEORGIA!" Nancy snapped.

"No. I didn't."

Immediately following these words, everyone in the courtroom looked at press like he was a crack-head walking fresh off of the streets to church on Easter Sunday. They were in a complete state of shock. Was this officer retarded? Or just stuck on stupid? They asked one another.

"I was saying that I didn't see him throw it on the ground," Press corrected, eliminating the possibility of any more misunderstandings.

"He threw it in the grass."

CHAPTER 18

Osta Lavista

The local media had a field day with the Eugene Shabazz case. After several days of reviewing the evidence, and additional testimonies, the jury rendered a guilty verdict. The charge itself wasn't a big deal. Traditionally, the city of Savannah witnessed crimes more horrific. But the political ties of this particular criminal changed the landscape of the way the media viewed petty crimes. This was the relative of the notorious Philo, an alleged member of the UAT, so this case was worth pursuing because it included advertisement and exposure.

Narc agent's Anderson and Mcgurt were commended tremendously for their supporting roles. Without the assistance of the feds the local narcotics department managed to take down the most influential trapper the city of savannah had ever seen, which was astronomical. This accomplishment gained the narcotics taskforce department the respect of all the other judicial branches of law enforcement. Dually, they helped weaken Philo's drug empire, and as a result, all the CNT agents in Captain Ranger's unit were promoted and viewed as heroes. Finally, the biggest buzz amongst the law enforcement community surrounded Rangers's unit and due to this he was eternally grateful.

"So how are you feeling?" Captain Ranger asked Press from behind his desk. He had some good news for Press, his favorite employee.

"I'm holding up."

"Sure you are. Son, you're a terrible liar. You're still beating yourself up about testifying on that piece of shit aren't you?" Captain Ranger quizzed. Then he reassured press that what he did was the right thing and he told him how much respect that he had for him because of the sacrifice that he made. According to Ranger, Press was honest, born with integrity, and overall, a good cop, and that's something that he didn't need to forget.

"O, and Aaah, Ranger said folding his arms as he sat back in the seat of his chair. Don't worry about filling out any paperwork. I'll fax all your information wherever you decide to transfer too. I got you covered buddie," Captain Ranger promised while giving press the thumps up.

After giving Press the week off, Press proceeded to leave. But he wasn't sure how he'd spend his vacation because Charlotte was mad at him for being dishonest in court.

"I really wish that you'd consider sticking with us Mcgurt. I know you want to get closer to home. I understand. But if I'm being completely honest, it's just not going to be the same around here without'cha. We'll miss you. I've grown kind of fond of having you around."

◆ ◆ ◆

The week passed by at a cheetah's pace. Charlotte packed her bags and left press in the house that they shared in the Garden City area. The Chief, Press's dad, was furious about the incident as well and refused to speak to him. Even Press's mom was mad at him for his testimony. The only difference is she didn't cease communication with him like the rest of his immediate family did. Eve, Adam, and Tandra never knew that Press lied during court. And even if they did, it was meaningless because this method of dishonesty amongst law enforcement officers was common. As far as the trio was concerned press was the police, so snitching and lyinig was a natural part of his profession.

Press thought that the feeling of regret would fade eventually. But this presumed emotion turned out to be futile. All he ever wanted to do is be like his dad. He just didn't need any handouts, and that's why he turned down the many opportunities that his dad provided, and ultimately, lied in court. Press wanted to independently establish his own name. This was the reason for his disobedience to his father. He wanted to be viewed by his peers as a professional. But now that he managed to accomplished that he wasn't too sure if that's what he really wanted. Why was his dad seemingly disapproving of every decision? Especially when considering how hard he worked? As a fellow officer, you'd think the chief would be more supportive.

Even tho they were some nice benefits that press reaped in exchange for his cooperation, he wasn't sure if his career was worth compromising his conscience and mental stability. The truth of the matter was no matter how much his subconscious mind tried to justify his behavior, deep down inside, press knew what he did was wrong and he'd have to live in shame, for the rest of his life, because he sent an innocent man to prison for twenty years + *Plus*

Regaining his identity, and conscienceness, Press awoke out of his train of thought. He, Agent Love, Anderson, and another agent were riding around in an unmarked car as usual exploiting the dope boys of the Seaport. None of them had heard or seen from Press since the day of the trial.

"I really appreciate you for having my back in that courtroom. I know we haven't spoke much since then. But I just wanted to say thanks," Narcotics Agent Anderson thanked press. He was sincere. If it wasn't for press's bravery he'd be out of a job right now.

The other narcs complimented press as well. He was worshipped and praised for his oscar worthy courtroom performance.

"You're my fuckin hero. Did you see the look on Sabastian's

face when you said, no, he threw it in the grass? Priceless. Tears were falling from his face. I thought it was incredible. Did you guys see the news headline? *"Senstive thug cries in courtroom."*

"You're not so tough now are you Eugene," the narc laughed diabolically, talking to no one in particular.

Agent Love was pondering to himself and he didn't say anything. The other two agents joked and boasted the entire ride but Agent Love was lost in deep thought. He always knew that there was more to Press than what met the eye. He knew that deep down inside, Press, was just like the rest of them, crooked, that's the real reason why he overlooked his hostility and sarcasm.

Press just needed a little time that's all. He'd come around. It took balls to do what Press did. And yeah, they had their differences, But press was solid. Noone else held such a stature, especially within their department. Press was a natural. He was the last of a dying breed.

◆ ◆ ◆

Taking it from the back, Nancy tightened her clit muscles and rocked her lower body back and forth forcing friction with Press's manhood. She was receiving the fuck of a lifetime and Press was exactly what the doctor ordered.

"Umm-hmm. Faster Press! Nancy demanded. DAMMIT PRESS. I SAID FASTER!" She ordered in an oblivious state of ecstasy.

Taking her advice, Press picked up his pace, going harder with each stroke. Nancy had fucked criminals for years. So tonight, Press would show her how it felt for once. With this in mind, press continued to multi-task, pounding and smacking Nancy's butt cheeks with the palm of his right hand. He was stroking simultaneously. A huge puddle of sweat found its way up his torso, eventually covering his naked body. This only enhanced the intensity between the two and forced the veins inside of his shaft to swell.

After a series of loud screams and orgasms, the newfound duo sat on nancy's bed and made small talk. They talked about their careers, hobbies, and dreams. Press told Nancy why Charlotte broke up with him and she shared sensitive info about her fiancé, who was a part-time lawyer/politician. He became a narcissist and verbally abusive ever since the sabastian case which skyrocketed her career much faster than his.

After Nancy's confessions, and they got dressed, she said. "You know Press. I know your still feeling bad about testiying. But trust me. What your feeling is normal. You're a good man Preston. And don't you *ever* forget that."

Nancy finished her speech, sat down beside press on the bed, and stared at the wall. "You know I oversentence people five days a week, fifty-two weeks a year. I know that the punishments for these crimes are to extreme. But my job is to hold these criminals accountable, even if it means enforcing misdermeaner penalties. I'm *extremely* good at negotiating," Nancy explained.

"Guys get arrested for drugs, sometimes for small portions, as little as 1 gram, and I force them into taking ten, and fifteen year sentences," Nancy confessed almost regretfully. When I started out, I was a lot like you, honest. But then I just became obsessed with the power that I had over those people that broke the law."

"I really do want the bad guys off the streets. But I know that arresting them is not always the best solution. The prison system in our country is a croc of shit. You, I, and the general public knows that much. Our faternity, the guys and gals who wear badges, know it too. I hear just how much of a piece of shit the judicial system is all time," Nancy said.

"But I can't let my emotions limit my career," Nancy added. Teary eyed, she stood and headed towards the exit. She didn't want Press to see her in such a vulnerable state.

Hanging up the phone, Press breathed a sigh of relief as he gathered his thoughts.

Thank god. I can't function without her.

After two weeks of begging charlotte for another chance, she finally decided to forgive him. However, she wasn't ready to come back home just yet. But press was fine with that. He didn't complain. Slow progress was better than none at all he figured.

Feeling guilty for having sex with Nancy, Press sat up in his lonely bed staring at the ceiling. The other day Nancy's words were as sharp as daggers piercing through the depths of his conscience. Criminals behaved like animals true enough. But did they deserve to be penalized for crimes they didn't commit? And even if they did do the crime, which *is* the case in most cases, the sentences are too lengthy and harsh when taking into account how petty the crimes are. The American justice system is supposed to rehabilitate criminals, not increase the probability that they'll commit another crime upon supervised release. The justice system doesn't provide any justice. Its the biggest scam and money hungry institution of them all.

After reaching this conclusion, Press started to question his own motives. Did he have a secret agenda that he always understood but chose to abandon? Did he become a cop for the wrong reasons? When someone told a lie, what did that mean? Lies was something that was exercised by everyone. The young, old, and rich. From a crack-head to a God-fearing Pastor, everyone shared that deceitful trait at some point in their lives. Some lies are harmless, while others effect feelings, relationships, and even some people's lives. Some are predictable. And others come unexpectedly. The foundation of America was based on a lie, Christopher Columbus didn't really discover this land. As the saying goes, the devil is a lie. So what did that make Press? His co-workers? The United States of American? The devil?

Press didn't have all the answers. But he did make a few promises to himself. From that day forth, he would never lie again to that extent. Starting tomorrow he planned to expose the liars simbly by telling the truth.

◆ ◆ ◆

The next day Press woke up earlier than usual to report to work. Today he had a real important task and he wanted to get an early start.

Entering the precinct, Press passed the team of narcs intentionally failing to greet its members. They were in the briefing room discussing Today's agenda.

Press ignored them and headed towards Captain Ranger's office.

"Look who decided to join us, my favorite narc. Good morning, Captain Ranger greeted. I have some good news for you bud. I was just about to call you. You must've read my mind," Captain Ranger said in a dry attempt to boost press's ego for the thousandth time.

After a few minutes of silence passed Captain Ranger resumed. "Here. That's your promotion. You deserve it. Read it."

Silence

"So what'da ya say? Don't just stare at the paper. Cheer up some y don't' cha."

"Congratulations."

Press pretended to be in a state of disbelief. Then he glanced down at the paper a second time. Sure enough it stated that he was being promoted to a sergeant. Not the least bit surprised, Press continued to read over his new job title.

"And the best part of it is that I'm assembling you a team. Your own team. From here you report to me. Not love. Your no longer apart of his crew. You're the boss. Next to me of course," the boss joked.

"I can get used to being the boss," Press confessed.

They made small talk. Captain Ranger told a few early morning jokes and kept reminding Press how much of a great leader he needed him to be now that he was being promoted to sergeant.

"So who do you have in mind? Dabage? Jackson? I have the perfect agent in mind. Williams. He'll fit perfectly under your command. I kn—

"Fuck you Ranger."

Ignoring press's comment, Captain Ranger continued to list different agents that he thought were best to work under Press.

"U deaf?" Press spat, ripping up the paperwork with his new position on it. He shredded it into small pieces and threw it at Ranger's face.

"I'm not fucking with none of them mufuckas because I'm through working for your racist ass. *CRACKA!"*

Shocked, Captain Ranger slammed his coffee cup against the ground until it broke. But this only made Press madder.

"Fuck' you ranger, white bitch. And that goes for all theses agents. Even the black ones that keep their noses up yo' ass. Yall aint no better than the dope boys yall hate so much *FUCK YALL!!!* Press yelled.

Nearing the exit door, Press turned around with no regrets, now facing his colleagues. He reached inside of his pants, pulled out a lighter, and sparked it, connecting the burning flames to his badge. He waited until most of it was covered in ashes and burnt crisp before tossing it to the ground.

CHAPTER 19

Black to the future

Over the next few weeks, Press kept a low profile. After hearing that he opted to quit his job, Charlotte moved back home. She knew that press was vulnerable and that he could use her support so she took off from work for a few weeks so they could rekindle the love that was nearly lost among them.

Press felt like a ton of bricks was lifted off his shoulders. Although he missed the excitement, he refused to be a part of a movement so toxic.

Sure, he could've chosen to take his dad up on his offer and worked in another department. But Press wanted to find his own way. Besides, he was through with law enforcement entirely. The laws were unjust as it was already the last thing society needed was a crooked cop to enforce them. What good would transferring do when the same type of toxicity went on in even higher places? If Nancy, the leading district attorney, was a part of such a conspiracy, surely this behavior could be found at the very top of the food chain. Lawyers, politicians, Judges, the government, and even previous presidents broke the law in some form of fashion. Whoever came up with the phrase *"It aint' a crime until you get caught" aint never lied.*

The rules didn't apply to people of significant power. But that's where the problem stood. The constitution is supposed to provide civilans with democracy, not hypocrisy. The amedments, much like the law, is supposed to guarantee protection, and liberty. Therefore, criminal behaviour shouldn't be found in any branch of Government.

Resuming his conversation with his mom, who was interrupting his thoughts for the past five mintues, Press continued to listen as she spoke.

The phone conversation went on for almost thirty minutes before she said what was really on her mind.

"So how do you plan on making things right with this sabastian boy's family?"

"I'm not sure ma. I went by his baby mom's house the other day and told her that I'd help if she needed anything. She thought I was hilarious."

"So she laughed at you? Predictable. I would've been worst," Ms. Clarrissa confessed making it more of a statement than a question.

"Things got pretty akward afterwards. Some litte girl, I'm guessing her daughter, tried to fight me. She didn't look a day over ten."

"I heard that you and your dad are on speaking terms again. Good luck," Ms. Clarissa teased switching the subject to lighten the mood.

Press's mom talked about Sabastian's family again. Afterwards, she gave him a lecture.

Sensing how uncomfortable the subject made press feel, she said.

"Well. Did you pray on it?"

"Every night."

"You did your job then son. Don't be too hard on yourself. You made a mistake, prayed on it, now move on. It's not like you could do it all over again. Because I'm sure if you could, you would."

Press pulled up in front of the historical building that sat on Abercorn Street. The building was every bit of two stories tall. Gold trimming surrounded the window shields. Even the lawn was impeccable and freshly cut, accompanied by a yellow brick road like sidewalk.

After talking with his mom, Press realized just how blessed he was to have her in his life. Her advice always proved to be accurate.

"I'm sure if you could, you would."

These words altered press's agenda as far as sabastian was concerned. His mom was right. If he could change the past he would and he'd prove it right here in this moment.

Once Press was inside the building, he greeted the secretary. She was a young blond with semi freckles on her face.

"Good afternoon."

"Good afternoon sir."

"Your boss in?"

"Umm. I think so. Can you hold for a sec hun?" The secretary exclaimed before picking up the telephone on her desk. She punched in a few numbers shortly after.

"Yes. Umm. I have a—what's your name hun?" She whispered. She and the receiver was lost in their own conversation.

"Preston Mcgurt."

"A Preston Mcgurt's here to see you. What—No—I said Preston —sure---Ok. I'll give her a call later. Chow," the secretary said pressing the button to end the conversation. Lifting her head, she started playing with her nails.

"Once you make it up the stairs, it'll be the first door on your right," the nonchalant secretary instructed.

◆ ◆ ◆

"Let me guess. You're here because Nancy wants to rub her victory in my fuckin' face," Attorney Ortega assumed.

"Nope," Press replied, curious about Ortega's question.

I wonder why he's so mad? Does he know that I slept with Nancy? Is he fuckin' her too?

"Good. Because I don't think I can handle anymore of those corney jokes. The fact that she keeps bragging about that case is annoying."

"That fuckin Shabazz case costed me some of my biggest clients. Can you believe it? Everyone seems to think that I'm useless because I couldn't get someone off for a petty drug charge. *Unfuckinbelievable*," attorney Ortega placed his hands on his forehead, continuing to complain.

Once attorney Ortega calmed down some, he said, "So who got caught with their hand in the cookie jar this time? That is why you're here right? One of you smucks stole a drug dealer's money again?"

"Actually, I came for something else.""

Proping his feet up on top of his laptop, Ortega look at the screen of his computer.

"I'm listening."

"I didn't see sabastian throw anything."

After thinking about Press's comment, Ortega clicked the left button on the computer's mouse.

"Conscience couldn't take it any more?"

Press shook his head. "I'm only human. I feel terrible," Press admitted, watching as attorney Ortega surfed the internet.

"So what now?"

"What the hell do you mean what now? You testified and got an innocent man twenty years remember? It's a little too late to have a heart now don't ya think?"

Ignoring Ortega's sarcasm, Press continued. He was focus and determine to finish what he started.

"What about the appeal?"

"O, Ortega mumbled, finally catching on. I see. You want to clear the record?"

"If I can. Sure."

"And you'll state this on record?"

"I wouldn't be here otherwise."

Sitting up, attorney Ortega shut down the operating system to his lap top. Then he said. "But what about your job? You're telling me that you're willing to give that up for a piece of shit like Eugene? That's a first," Ortega was impressed.

"I'm flying solo these days. I quit."

"Another first. I mean, what are you, a fuckin unicorn?"

"Look robin hood. I'd love to help. But you'll have to consult with Eugene's new lawyer, Scottie. I'm no longer his attorney. The motherfucker fired me. Said I manipulated him. A fuckin multi-million-dollar drug dealer, manipulated. *Unfuckinbelievable,*" Ortega repeated.

After hearing how Eugene's dumb ass shoulda took the plea for the thousandth time, Press thanked Ortega for his help. Then, he collected Scottie's information and left.

CHAPTER 20

"Here you go Ike, eat this"

"To new beginnings," Press proposed, clinging champagne glasses with the love of his life, Charlotte. They were at a new restaurant celebrating the fact that he landed a job at a Bank of America.

"You're a trip bae. Look at you wasting it all over yourself. You don't even know how to drink," Charlotte teased.

"Tusha. You wanna come lick it off?"

"Hell-to-the-nawl."

They bursted out laughing in unison. Charlotte barely used profanity. But that's what made her comment amusing. And ghetto.

In the midst of them entertaining each other, a light skin man walked up to their table and interrupted. He sported gold, had a temp-fade, and stood nearly 6'feet tall.

"Sup?"

"Sup bro."

"coolin," the stranger replied, taking a seat despite not receiving permission.

"Excuse you. We had a reservation and the waiter assigned *us* this table. So if you don't mind me and my man would like some privacy."

Ignoring Charlotte, the light skin fella rolled his eyeS. Then he focused on press.

"You don't remember me?"

"Bro. I'm here with my girl. I don't want any trouble. But I'm strapped. I have a registered firearm."

"I meant no disrespect."

"You really don't remember me do you? Tatumville? Remember? Me and that crazy broad who pushed your partner?"

"Press nodded even tho the guy didn't look familiar.

"How's she doing?"

"Don't know. Don't fuck with her anymore. I know you still don't remember me. You want your privacy and I can respect that. I'll never forget what you did for me. I owe you big-time bros."

They talked for ten more minutes mostly about politics and sports. Then the man thanked Press for the twentieth time, gave him his number, and left.

Visibly irritated, Charlotte breathed a sigh of relief. "Thank god. You guys know you can talk about sports. Especially him. *Rude ass.*"

◆ ◆ ◆

The next night Press found himself sitting at home practically bored to death as he juggled with his thoughts. Charlotte was currently at a birthday party. She wanted him to come as well but he declined the invite.

Hell I look like hanging with a bunch a women? A sissy. No, I made the right decision.

On a quest to rid the problem of boredom, he made an attempt to contact Officer Daniels. They remained friends even tho he was no longer on the force. Coinsidently, he received the voice mail. Then he remembered the number that the guy had given him that day at the restaurant. Why not he thought. What did he have to lose? Before making actual contact, he gave the idea some thought. Upon further examination of the piece of paper, he remembered where he knew the guy from.

Dat's rite, Trick. That's his name. That's what the girl kept calling him back then. At the time, I just thought it was her bashing him. But it turns out that dat was really his name. I followed my gut and let him go free, that's why he wants to hang. Maybe I'll take him up on that offer.

"Hello," Trick answered in a simi rude tone.

"Sup?"

"Who dis?"

"Press."

"Press? I'on kno no Press. You got the wrong number."

"They call you Trick. Don't they? This is officer Mcgurt. Or should I say ex officer. Remember? The guy from the restaurant?"

"Ooo. Robocop. You should've said that in the beginning. Sup wit'cha?"

They conversated for a few minutes exchanging life stories. Tricks parents were strung out on dope and he had a four-year-old daughter from some nasty stripper. This was just some of the things that Trick shared with Press.

"So wyd?"

"Wyd. I don't get it."

"It means what you doing. You're the police and you don't kno the social media lingo. Pathetic."

"Ex police."

"Same thing. So check it. Send me the address. I'm on my way to get you. We're going out tonight. So start getting dressed."

"Who said anything about me leaving?"

"You did when you told me your girl went to some party and left you. I'm on the way. So Imma need you to cut off porn-hub and take your dick from out of the palm of your hands. You on my timeline now. You can masterbate later," Trick joked.

In no time Trick arrived at Press's house. He pulled into the driveway and waited for press inside of the car.

"Dam cuzzin. This you? Yall living like kings. This house big as shit. What I got to do to be the police?"

"Smoke weed, and rob drug dealers."

"This is true. And why are you dressed like we still in the seventies? Go back in there and change. You aint following me looking like that Ike Turner."

"You don't know nothing about this boy. This is polo. And why you keep calling me cuzizn? We aint kin," Press said in a state of confusion not understanding the c-port slang.

Following a brief conversation and change of wardrobe, they jumped back inside of Trick's car and headed to their destination. Press was dress to impress. He had on a button up polo shirt (an updated version this time), blue denim jeans, and a pair of low top cohans..

"So what club are we headed to? Frozen?"

"An officer that likes to party in the jungle? I'm impressed. They been shut that bitch down. Spot now is Island Breeze. Sorry Tarzan."

Island Breeze was a mello club located on Savannah's west side. It was the number one place where teens and adults alike gathered to celebrate.

Once inside the club, they made their way to the bar. Trick ordered a few bottles of ciroc and they posted in the back of the club. Then Trick grabbed two random females and they headed towards the dance floor.

The female that chose Press started shaking her ass harder

than anyone he ever seen. This girl would put the singer Ciara to shame. She started wiggling her butt cheeks and dipping it low. Gyrating her hips, the girl turned around so that she could face Press, rubbing her pelvis against his rock-hard crotch. The DJ was playing young Jeezy's song but you would've thought that it was Juvenile's the way that she was backing dat ass up. Drunker than six sailors, Press was loving every bit of it. His date for the night was extremely gorgeous and flirtatious. Standing 5'5, she was built like a stallion.

Press ignored all incoming calls that night, especially Charlotte's. And this female's body was the reason. Her juicy lips and perfectly rounded ass was a distraction.

I'm too drunk to face Charlotte tonight. Maybe I'll stay out late. But what am I going to tell her when she asks why I haven't answered? My phone went dead. Yup. That's the perfect excuse.

After the club, they skated back to one of Tricks trap-houses. They weren't even in the house for a full ten minutes before the events listed below took place.

"Let me holler at you for a minute bro's," Trick waved, signaling Press over. Once he arrived, Trick reached inside of his pants and pulled out a plastic bag.

"Here you go Ike. Eat this."

Press shook his head.

"Cuzzo. Them hoes that we just brought home's rolling, meaning they on some potent pills. Mollies, xans, and ecstasy. Makes them horny. And we can't keep up unless we indulge. Just relax. And don't be so uptight. You aint the police nomore. Lighten up robocop."

"Please dirtie. I need your help. I can't fuck both of them hoes by myself, Trick complained."

Thinking about Trick's comment, Press stared at the pills with a blank expression on his confused face. Back when he was a narcotics agent, they'd confiscate pills occasionally. Agent

Love always bragged about his ability to satisfy women after taking the pills. The rumors went like this: Men, that pop pills, usually gained friends, favortism, and stamina.

After a few minutes of battling with his conscience, Press decided to move forward. Why not? He asked himself. He just couldn't think of a good enough reason not to partake.

Trick and Press returned to the bedroom following consumption. Shortly thereafter the predictions surrounding drug usage came into floushing. Afterwards, the guys were *favored* by the ladies. They formed *friendship*s after having countless hours of "*amazing sex.*"

◆ ◆ ◆

Over the next few weeks Press and Trick became besties. They hung out at bars, played pool together, and even borrowed each others clothes.

Trick was a cool guy in Press's opinion. Sure, he broke the law. But so did his ex co-workers, and they were cops. Selling dope didn't make trick a bad person. Furthermore, it wasn't like he was the one partaking in any illegal activities. Press witnessed his co-workers break the law first hand, for nearly eighteen months, so this wasn't a big deal in comparison. Periodically, Trick's customers would meet them at mysterious locations to purchase drugs. But Trick's choice of profession wasn't any of Press's business. Trick was his homey, and homies didn't abandon each other regardless if they made different career choices.

They were having a conversation in Tricks car while heading to Auto Zone. Since Press downgraded from a Narcotics agent to a bank employee, his fixed salary decreased tremendously. He traded in the brand-new truck that he bought for a used one, the car payments was kicking his ass. Not to mention the mortgage to his home in Garden City. Good thing Charlotte was still a probation officer and could help endure the financial burden. Otherwise, they'd be living inside of a cardboard box.

After discovering that his car battery was dead that morning at work Press called Trick. Charlotte wasn't available. She had a doctor's appointment.

"On the real cuzzin, Trick said puffing on a cigarette. One of his hands was on the steering wheel and the other was holding nicotine. Yo' cuzin set a lot of mufuckas up out of town. There's a hefty tickect on her head," Trick informed. They just picked up the battery and they were heading back to Press's car now.

"Didn't know dat."

"Figures. Me, Adam, and Eve went to school together. And word get around."

Press just sat there and played dumb as if he hadn't heard these rumors a million times already. Trick was a great friend. But family secrets was off limits and not "*everyone's business.*"

"Does she have life insurance? Because she's a dead bitch. Can' u say *"free money,"* Trick joked, making fun of press's cousin.

They chopped it up, laughing and joking the whole time. Press decided against telling Trick that his dad was the Chief of police. Reason being, if Trick made fun of his cuzin, a cold hearted criminal, he could only imagin what type of wise-cracks that would come if trick knew who his father was. If trick was ever privy to this information a comedic session would soon follow.

They were near Press's truck the next time either spoke.

"So wasup with ol girl? You told her what I said?"

Press nodded.

"I hope you gave her my number like I asked?"

"Don't even come at me like dat cuzzin," Press defended, having mastered using the c-port slang now. Unbeknownst to him, Trick was starting to rub off on him.

Why does he keep asking me about people who work with me? First it was Tonya. Then it was Lisa. Now Melissa. I hope he's not planning to do what we did that night with them chics from island breeze. He knows I'm trying to be faithful.

After having these thoughts, they reached Press's truck, put the battery in, dapped each other up, and went their separate ways.

CHAPTER 21

The End

"Check," Noble Drew Ali said as he placed his bishop in front of Press's king. They were engaged in a intense game of chess and there was only a few more moves left until checkmate.

"Checkmate, once again. That's three times in a row son. I guess the third time's not a charm."

Every since press quit the force, he had a lot of extra time on his hands. So more often than not he came on 34th street between Barnard and Whitaker to play chess and checkers with the old school guys from the community. One guy in particular, Noble Drew Ali, became one of his closest confidant's. Like Trick, they talked about everything, including Charlotte, and he rarely sought relationship advice from anyone outside of his immediate family. He even shared the fact that his dad was the Chief of police with the older fella, which was a first, and something that he didn't even do with Trick for security purposes. The two of them didn't just share chess matches, they shared stories, forming a bond that was growing rapidly each day.

The Moorish Science Temple of America is an American national and religious organization founded by Noble Drew Ali. He was an advocate for America's *"alleged"* terrorist group, the sovereign citizen movement. Drew believed that African Americans are descended from the Moors of North West Africa and thus were Moorish by nationality and Islamic faith. Ali put together elements of major traditions to develop a message of personal transformation through historical education, racial pride, and spiritual upliftment. His doctrine was intended to provide African Americans with a sense of identity in the world and to promote civic involvement. All African Americans are of Moorish ancestry, specifically from the Moorish Empire. This area included other countries that today surrounds Morocco. To join the movement, individuals had to proclaim their Moorish nationality. Then they were given nationality cards.

After explaining these things to press, they presumed their chest match. Press was extremely competitive. He hadn't won a game since the day they met.

"So you telling me that you're Moorish American?"

"Precisely. And so is every black person here in the United States."

"But I'm not affiliated with the Moorish Science Temple if that's what you're asking. The name was given to me by a fellow member who happens to be a good friend of mind. Said I resembled the guy."

"So where's this Noble Drew guy now?"

"He died from tuberculosis broncho-pneumonia, according to our government. But it's rumored that he was murdered. By the police department."

"Some people just don't get enough," Press said watching some kid across the street hand a smoker a piece of crack. For the past ten minutes they silently observed drug transactions that was made by the neigborhood fiends and a few teenage misfits.

"That CNT raid from earlier was useless. Didn't help anything. These kids will never stop. The show must go on. U of all people should know that," Noble Drew Ali replied.

Then they played a few more games of chess before Press went home. He had an important task tomorrow and he needed to prepare for work in the morning.

◆ ◆ ◆

Later that night, Press settled down and tried to relax a little. He hopped out of the shower just minutes before and he was now watching sports center on ESPN. Lebron James was the center of the highlights.

"Bae. We need to talk," Charlotte whispered, as she sat down on the couch beside him.

"I'm all ears."

"Are you still hanging with Trick?"

"Charlotte. Please don't start."

"I'm just concerned Press, she voiced. He sells dope bae. Dope. It's only a matter of time before he gets caught. And I'm scared."

"I'm trying to watch the game man. Please. Can I watch?" Press replied, visibly irritated.

"What you need to do is think bae. Just here me out. What if your in the car with him and yall get red flagged? Cause he has drugs? What then? You'll go down with him right? Of course you will. You of all people should know that dope boys don't last long in this business."

"I know that's your friend and everything bae but he's a bad influence on you. He shouldn't be selling drugs when your around," Charlotte preached, urgently attempting to make press severe his ties.

"Can't he wait until y—

"Do I say anything when you out partying with your fuckin friends all time of night? Hun Clarissa? That is who you think you are rite, my mom? News flash. No the fuck you aren't. Your name, is Charlotte, a fuckin spoiled brat. And constant pain in my ass."

"Am I all down your throat about your crack smoking father? Now that's a real junkie. That mothafucka's a bad influence on you too then. How about you stay *AWAY FROM HIM!*"

"FUCK YOU PRESS!!! Charlotte yelled in tears. Now she was hurt. In five whole years Press never spoke to her like that. Especially about her dad.

"That man does more shit for me that you! Press snapped. You're just mad because I'm hanging out with him instead of your nagging ass!"

Crying like a baby, Charlotte walked towards their bedroom to grab her purse. But that didn't faze Press. It only made him madder.

"And you know why I don't spend that much time with you no more? Take a guess?" He questioned, using sarcasm, right before charlotte reappeared. She had her purse and car keys. She was leaving.

"Because every time I wanna *fuck* you be too tired, or busy suckin' the government's dick!"

"Shit. Trying to tell me who I can and can't hang out with like you somebodys mom. *Must be out yo rabbit ass mind.*"

Crying hysterically, Charlotte stormed out the door with a brokenheart. But this time, she wan't coming back. Ever.

CHAPTER 22

Trick or treat

Two months past and Charlotte and Press was still not speaking. This time it was over. For good.

After the fight, Charlotte came back to the house to collect the rest of her things and press hadn't heard from her since. As far as he was concerned it could stay that way. Five years was a long time to be invested in a relationship. But Charlotte was too controlling. She wanted to replace his mom, and that was the center of their problem. Sure, he was blowing caution to the wind by hanging with Trick. But he felt like he was an ex cop, not a fool. But apparently, charlotte thought so. Press was an honest man but he wasn't naïve about his flaws. Since Charlotte couldn't accept his imperfections, her decision to leave was best for them both. Nobody's perfect.

Getting back to reality, Press took another sip of his orange juice. He and Noble Drew Ali was lost in a deep conversation. They had already played a few games of chess and now they were chilling.

"Press. You don't look to good."

"Long night.."

"I'm not sold. I was just talking for a whole hour but u wasn't listening. I betcha u can't tell me what I said."

"O I heard you loud and clear. You said you wanted your ass beat again. Cool. Put your money where your mouth is pops."

They both laughed a little at Press's comment.

"You miss her hun?"

"Miss her? Me? Spshh. The same cunt that think she's my mom? I'll pass."

Feeling a potential argument arising, Noble Drew Ali changed the subject. He knew Press was lying. He had been making negative remarks about Charlotte all day and NDA knew those love jones symptoms all to well.

"So. Like I was saying. So when I come to the house, angel and her fine ass sister's laying in the bed butt booty naked..."

Noble Drew Ali (NDA) continued to tell Press one of his childhood stories. They laughed continuously, mostly about Drew's stories. Drew was an undercover comedian.

After a series of stories, NDA got up to leave. He had on a white tank top that complimented his well-built frame. Press also noticed that Noble Drew had a tattoo on the left side of his shoulder. Prior to this moment, he had'nt seen it before.

Press inspected further and nearly collapsed. This revelation was shocking. His mind had to be playing tricks he thought. This wasn't possible. *Or was it.*

There were rumors sorrunding the three lettered word that was attached to Drew's skin. High profile rumors.

Press shook his head in utter disbelief.

I must be seeing things. I probably need glasses.

Press had heard so much rumors surrounding the organization printed on Noble Drew Ali's arm. Political figures such as campaign managers, judges, cops, and even some religious pastors were rumored to be linked to this secret society of criminals. The word was that this society ruled with an iron fist and was formed by a slew of wealthy blacks after the Rodney king beating. Eventually, the organization expanded into the south amercia territory. This move formed an alliance with the Puerto Ricans and Columbians. As the story goes, the organization was in direct competition with the lacost the nostra, battling and extorting the legend Italian mafia for jobs. The Mexican cartel rumors came a lot later.

Press found it shocking that he didn't know such an intricate part of his friend's real identity. He wanted to inquire more about it. But for fear of rejection and reasons unknown he decided against it.

In this very moment this ex narc became aware of one thing. One very important thing. The UAT "*did*" exist, his quit wit and eyes lead him to that conclusion. And so the rumors were true. The UAT moved in secrecy. And They controlled everything. Including chessboards.

◆ ◆ ◆

Press returned to work that following day. Today it was Monday, and he was still feeling the effects from his hangover. He and Trick had multiple threesomes with several females, which was becoming a thing of the norm for the duo. They sexed, smoked, and experimented every position known to man that weekend.

"Why does everyone look like their mom just died?" Press asked, glancing around his work space, bank of america. His co-workers, Melissa, and everyone else seemed to be out of place for some odd reason.

"Hmm. You haven't heard?" Melissa replied sarcastically rolling her eyes and sucking her teeth. She looked him in the eyes and studied his face.

"Heard what?"

"We got robbed Friday."

"*Getdafuckoutahere. You lying?*"

"Wish I was."

After bringing Press up to speed and giving him an exaggerated account, (as most black folks do), he was called to the back office. The FBI agents and the owner were conducting an investigation and Press was one of many who had to be interrogated.

"So I'm guessing you heard that we were robbed?" The owner wasted no time questioning Press once he entered the room.

Press nodded his head.

"Just got briefed by Melissa."

Witnessing the two interact, the detective who'd been hired for the case stepped in. "Do *you* have any clue why it happened or who did this?"

Shocked, Press felt uneasy answering the question.

How the fuck am I suppose to know? I just got to work.

Press shook his head.

Expecting Press's response, the detective used the remote control to turn on the flat-screen TV monitors. The cameras that were affixed to the ceiling captured the entire robbery from every angle.

Press watched as the screen flashed on. There was two men that ran inside the bank. One carried an AK47 and the other a nine-millimeter. The man with the nine fired warning shots immediately. He then rushed the bank teller and slapped her with the pistol, right before making her take him to the back where the safe was hidden. Out of the cameras view at this point, the only visible robber during this time was Mr. AK47. And he made everybody lay down and face the floor just minutes before this. Waving the AK47, he screamed something but because of the lack of audio no one could hear it. Whatever he was yelling, it included the words Imma and Kill. The guy's lip movement confirmed that much.

One of the hostages was receiving a real brutal beating. He made it halfway to the ground. But apparently, he wasn't moving fast enough.

BOP! BOP! BOP! BOP!!! The innocent man was slapped across the face with the butt of the Assault rifle. A massive blood trail found its way down his face in seconds.

By now the robber's accomplice was resurfacing on video. Four duffle bags stuffed with money occupied his hands. The bags were filled to the top. Every time the robber moved, another dollar bill dropped as a result.

The fourth camera captured a perfect shot of one of them before they exited the bank. A ball cap covered his eyes, but the rest of his face was cleary visible. Anyone who knew the man could recognize him despite the inconspicuousness.

Shocked, Press convinced himself that the man with the bags in his hands wasn't who he thought it was. And even if it was, it wasn't any of his business. Whatever happened was between *that* person and the bank.

"Recognize any of them?" The detective asked as they all watched the robbers leave the bank on video. The monitors were rolling the hostages reaction to the tragedy. Everybody rushed to the man's aid who was beaten with the Assault rifle.

Press shook his head.

"You sure?"

"Of course. Wish I could help. But I can't. Sorry."

Hearing Press's words, the detective rewined the tape back to the moment when the fourth camera captured the robber with the baseball cap. He then stood up and folded his arms. "I think you're lying Mr. Mcgurt. I think you know exactly what happened. Your co-worker seems to think so. Melissa. You do know *"her"* don't you?" The federal detective mocked sarcastically during his interrogation.

"From what I've been hearing, you and *this* guy, the detective continued to accuse, pointing forcefully at the screen. Are real good buddies."

"Care to explain?"

CHAPTER 23

Too many Indians, not enough Chiefs

For the next couple of days Press's world turned upside down. He continued to reach out to Trick but to no avail. He even stopped by some of Trick's hangouts spots, but no-one seemed to know Trick's government name, or about his whereabouts. It was almost as if Trick disappeared off the face of the earth. But the most disrespectful part about it was Trick's lack of consideration for Press's wellbeing, his so-called compadre and homeboy. In Press's eyes, the ultimate betrayal came when Trick robbed the bank without giving him a heads up.

As it stood currently Press was being charged with being a accessory to the robbery. And to make matters worse, his co-worker, Melissa, spotted Trick first on the visual camera and informed the detective upon this observation. That, along with Trick's antics caused a shift in Press's attitude.

Snitch bitch Melissa. O God. If your real, and really do answer prayers, I need a favor. I pray that bitch gets hits by a bus. And not a regular bus either. One of those, big ass, stupid cat buses. Amen.

After the depletion of Press's meditation, he reflected on Trick's betrayal. The realization that his so-called friend deceived him hurt. Trick was a snake, slizzering and crawling his way into Press's heart. But for some unknown reason he just couldn't figure out how he hadn't seen this coming.

How could I be so naïve? Wasn't I taught to never trust a criminal during my stay at the academy? I misused that information. Charlotte tried to warn me too. My dum ass.

In the streets of the C-pote, there were no rules. The strong often preyed on the weak, and the weak usually prayed on Sunday. But Press learned a valuable lesson from Trick's treachery. Never trust your friends. *Especially the ones with syllables in their names like "Trick."*

Still mad, Press thought about how much time he would be facing and nearly fainted. He was played for a fool. But when the opportunity presented itself, he'd show Trick just how much of a fool he really was. These were the vows that he made to himself and God.

Judge Juliet had a no-nonsense type of attitude. He very seldom gave pre-trial attendee's a break, he only gave lengthy sentences.

Practically disgusted with the case before him, Judge Juliet left his chambers. An ex-cop was taking a negotiated plea for being an accessory to a bank robbery. The mere notion had him pissed.

"All rise," the bailiff ordered. As the gallery stood, the judge entered the courtroom. The sentencing process began shortly thereafter.

After sentencing, the Chief of Police and Press's lawyer met up in the lobby. Press had just stepped out to the restroom at this point.

"Gosh, Attorney Russo said as he wiped the sweat that poured from his face. The government was pushing for five years, and 99.9% of the time, Judge Juliet coincides with whatever the prosecutor recommends. How'd you pull *that* off? Sheez. Remind me to call you if I'm in trouble," Attorney Russo joked.

"I have my resources," The Chief replied evasively.

Leaving the courthouse, the Chief of Police hopped in his awaiting squad car in disbelief.

God-dam lawyers. Tons of idiot's. I see they're accepting retards in law school now. You don't need a brain to pass the bar exam. Just coke, and a open nostril.

After bringing up names of certain political influences who contributed to his election as Judge, Julie agreed to let Press off with supervised probation. There was something surprisingly true about the saying that goes it's not about what you know, it's about what you can prove, and The Chief of police's black mailing tactic laid foundation to that claim.

Thinking about his son now, the Chief of police recalled back on the conversation that they shared just minutes ago. Press found a job at some local gas station. He was happy with it he said. But the Chief wasn't buying the fantasy tickets that Press was selling. The discomfort in his voice was obvious.

Although the Chief was disappointed in Press's career choices, he had to admit, he admired his son's strength. The Chief reminisced about the time when Press watched the guy named Smoke rob the store nearly twenty years ago. As a kid, you'd think that witnessing an event so tragic would hinder the child's ability to function. But the reversed effect was true. The tragedy made the child even badder. Press, at the age of seven, was beaten by his Dad after frustrating his teacher and interrupting class. Apparently, little press had been bragging about the robbery in school the next day despite the vow that he made with his dad to sworn secrecy.

Forwarding his son's life into adult-hood, the chief remembered the first day press attended the police academy. As usual, he had discouraged the move. But Press was extremely stubborn, and determined to follow in his footsteps by securing a career in criminal justice.

Press was a stand-up guy in the Chief opinion. Thats why he was so angry after the trial, because he knew that Press didn't possess a deceitful bone in his body. The Chief also dispised his son's boss, Ranger, because the chief knew that he inspired the charade.

You'll figure it out sooner or later son. I know you will. Failure's not in our blood.

These thoughts crowded the Chief's mind for hours.

CHAPTER 24

DePRESSed

Within no time six months passed since the day that Press began work at the local BP station. During that short period of time things went from worse to worser. Press was devestated thanks to a career reduction and lawyer fees. His financial burden began to overstay its welcome. He used to feel like he was on top of the world. But now it was as if the world was on top of him. He lost the home that he and Charlotte had worked so hard for. It sold during an auction. Foreclosure. Press couldn't maintain the bills all by himself, with no help, especially the mortgage. Now, he was living in a small apartment. He also had to trade in his used truck for a older model.

Leaving the convenience store, Press walked towards his unattrative truck. He grabbed himself a couple of beers and he was heading home.

"Press. Dat you? I could spot dat peanut ass head anywhere," Narc Love greeted, hopping out of the driver's seat of a brand-new beamer.

"Long time no see."

"Ikr."

Embarrassed, and using the latest social meeting slang, Press approached Agent Love with a simi genuine smile, praying that he hadn't noticed what kind of car he was driving.

"Dat's you?" Press pointed.

"Wat? This ol thing. Its nice rite? I bought it weeks ago. Aint it clean?" Agent Love bragged.

They made small talk. Then Agent Love offered to buy Press lunch and surprisingly he agreed to it.

Why not? I'm not doing shit anyway. These beers can wait. I hate this feeling. He's large. And Imma' fuckin bum.

Having these insecure thoughts and feeling sorry for himself, Press followed Agent Love to his immaculate beamer. Love entered the store and returned prior to their conversation.

"I'm glad you riding with me because dat truck isn't a good look. You need to take dat shit back to the junkyard. Asap. That's not cute Press. Not cute at all."

Morroco's was a new restaurant located in Savannah's historical downtown area. The scenery was exquisite. Gold chandeliers dangled from the ceiling matching the ensembles that complimented the walls, which were all gold too. The pictures were that of Dr. Martin Luther King, Malcom X, and other influential black leaders. The place was obviously owned by a descendant of the African diaspora.

After sitting, Agent Love got straight to the point. He wasn't thinking about press until today. Yet his desire to converse was so strong that he forgot to grab the menu.

"You know I'm not the type that beat around the bush. So dig this. I know Charlotte left you. And some petty criminal that you befriended got you fired from your job at the bank because he robbed the shit. You're on probation now, working at some pathetic gas station. Your barely making minimum wage. All the shit that you just told me on the way over here is laughable."

"How does he know all this?" It's what your thinking? Right? I got ears Press.

Press was beyond mad. Love's sarcasm angered him and only made things worse.

"You don't know shit! You think you know me? U got me all figured out, stop it. Phony ass. I been wanting to SMACK THE SHIT OUT CHU!" Press yelled slamming his glass on the able. The whole restaurant just stopped and stared at the ex-co-worker duo. WTF the crowd full of observers asked themselves.

"I know you riding around in that beat-up truck I saw you in earlier. I know you aint staying in that nice house you bought when you were law enforcement, I know dat much. *Bloodclaat Pussy boi.*"

Agent Love stood defensively. He threw his guards up. He was highly offended by Press's response.

After they calmed down, the waiter came and cleaned the broken glass. But it was Love who *broke* the silence.

"Look man. It aint like that bruh. I know that your frustration is not because of what I said, it's because of your situation. So Imma be the bigger man and apologize. My bad."

"All I was trying to do was get you to see that maybe, just maybe, you made a mistake by quiting the force. You and Charlotte didn't want for nothing when you were CNT. Am I lying?" Agent Love asked rhetorically.

"And look at you now, agent love mocked, shaking his head in disgust.

"Pitiful."

"See that's what I was trying to get you to understand in the beginning. You gotta stay ahead of the game. Sometimes, you gotta go against the grain in order to gain. Sometimes, especially when you're a black man in American, you gotta step outside of the box to prevent yourself from staying inside of one," Agent Love preached.

Receiving no feedback, he continued. Anyway man. I'm not here to brag, or throw my success in your face. I know that's what you think. But I genuinely want to help. Mainly because I know that you're one of the good guys. And I say that despite all the differences that we've had in the past."

"So here's what I'll do. You listening? I'll talk to Ranger about getting you back on the squad. He was extremely pissed after you cursed him out. But that was ages ago. Now I'm he's willing to let bygons be bygons."

◆ ◆ ◆

Later that night, Press found himself laying in his bed alone. After drinking the six pack of beer, it seemed like his head was starting to spend one hundred miles per hour.

I need to stop drinking these cheap beers. I'm killing myself. Got me pissing every fucking five minutes.

After coming from the restroom, Press cut off the lights and placed his clothes on the three-legged coffee table that he bought during a flea market sale. In the meantime, Agent Love's words were ringing inside of his head.

You gotta go against the grain in order to gain. You gotta step outside of the box, in order to prevent yourself from being inside of one.

That's exactly what his small apartment had become, a box, a fucking cardboard box. He also thought about his dad's advice a long time ago. "When shit hits the fan, turn on the AC." This one quote changed press's life. And for the very first time, he agreed with Love's reasoning. His life was pathetic. But he decided to do something about it right then and there.

CHAPTER 25

"Looks like its about to rain"

The next morning Press was up bright and early. He requested a day off just to take advantage of this opportunity.

"So you came to get beat down early this morning? Don't have anything to do?" Noble Drew Ali joked.

"I don't. I had a date with your baby mom's but she was on her period," Press replied jokingly. He walked into a chess match that was taking place already. Noble Drew Ali and another guy was in the middle of a very silent and intense game.

After nearly half of hour passed, Press sat down to the table replacing the losing opponent. After this happened, NDA pulled out a Cuban cigar and lit it. This kind of random behavior was his daily routine.

"Hey son. You're not tired of losing yet? This the tenth game you lost in a row," Noble Drew challenged.

Ignoring Noble Drew's comment, Press sat up.

"I need a favor," he blurted.

"If it's another loan, the answer's no. You already borrowed enough money this week."

Seeing that Press wasn't joking, NDA sat on the back hinges of his chair and relit the foreign cigar.

"I'm all ears."

"I need job."

"And you're telling me this because?"

"Because I know that you can help me get the type of job that I want."

Press held his breath before he spoke again. He chose his words carefully. "Look Drew. You've known me for months. And yea, I use to be a cop. But the game has changed, and so have I. I'm a grown man with bills, and your like a father to me. Your the only person on this planet I'd feel comfortable enough to ask of such a request."

"I know your apart of the UAT. And I need an opportunity. Not a handout. But an opportunity."

"Now before you say anything, Press held up his hand in an attempt to cut Noble Drew Ali off before he spoke.

"Know that this conversation, relationship, and every aspect of our friendship's exclusive. Everything that we discuss here is confidential."

"I can't help you."

"Look, I know what your thinking. But it's not like that anymore. You been knowing me for a while. I'm not the fucking police."

"I seen the tattoo you got Drew. Plus, every Wednesday around six a clock, you meet up with them at St. Paul's church on Barnard Street. I see your car parked ova there all the time."

"Never heard of them," NDA said as he stood to leave.

"That's bullshit! You think I like working at a fuckin gas station? YOU THINK I'M CONTENT WITH NOT HAVING SHIT!" Press screamed, angriliy and accusingly.

"Never fucking heard of them!" Noble Drew Ali yelled in response, slamming his frail hands on the table knocking over the chest pieces.

"NI GET THE FUCK OUT MY FACE!" NDA snapped.

Press was pissed. Mad at the world. Mad at Noble Drew Ali for thinking that he was still on some police shit. Hell, mad for no reason. Without saying another word, Press got up and walked off angrily. But not before breaking the table that once stood between him and his former friend.

A few days later, Press was bored out of his unstable mind. Today was just another day at work for him, and this had him feeling extremely depressed. He tried to listen to the radio. It didn't help. The only thing that could've brightened his day at this point was a bottle of hennesy.

Going to the licker store after work was a perfect way for press to escape his very sad and dull reality. Press was living paycheck to paycheck. He was also the owner of a raggedy, busted, pick up truck, and he lived in a roach infested apartment.

"Twenty on pump three," some immature white teen with blond hair said bringing him back into reality. The boy's face was full of joy. And radiant.

"How are you?" The kid asked, after collecting his change.

"I'm aiight."

"O," the kid replied, picking up on Press's attitude.

Placing the change in his pants pockets, the boy looked at the sky. "Jeez. It sure looks like it's about to rain. What do u think?"

"I disagree. You don't see how sunny it is out there?"

"No."

Press didn't find the kids response amusing.

"It was a joke."

Press ignored the boy as he tapped his fingers against the cash register.

Ok. You got your change. Now leave motor mouth so I can get back to feeling sorry for myself.

"Don't you just love young jezzy?"

"Wat?"

"I said, don't you just love young jezzy. The guy that you're listening to on the radio?"

"Mmm-hmm," Press replied, evasively, as he watched someone else step in the line to pay for gas.

It's about time. Dam. Be gone freckles.

"You like to swim?"

"Look lil man. There's somebody behind you waiting to get gas," Press blurted impatiently.

"Just answer the question. You swim?"

"No!!!" Press yelled, visibly irritated.

"At five thirty, when you get off, head to Tybee Island, and I mean the very second that you get off. When you hit the beach, take this to the guy that has on a pink shirt and shorts," the kid informed handing Press a piece of paper. And just like that, freckles disappeared.

Ignoring the customer's request for gas, Press opened the letter and started to read. The letter read Preston Mcgurt Jr, son of Preston and Clarissa Mcgurt. A long list of his relatives was also listed. It even contained information pertaining to Charlotte and his relationship, and the two of them had been separated for months until recently.

Sticking the paper in his pocket, Press tried to make some sense out of what transpired. It was obvious. The paper was confirmation letting him know that his family would be killed if this was a set up.

Noble Drew Ali proved to be a good friend after all. Because not only was he helping press out during this financial crisis, he was also given him a brand new identity and life.

◆ ◆ ◆

Once Press arrived on the beach, he looked for the guy that the kid described immediately. He couldn't wait to find him.

After nearly twenty minutes passed, Press finally discovered that there was actually no guy dressed in pink. This caused him to curse inside of his head.

The lil mufucka lied. I don't see anyone on this beach with pink.

Pissed, Press went to the hot dog stand not far away from the beach. Hopefully, he'd see him after he pleased his appetite. Maybe he was a little to late. The kid did say five thirty. But he managed to reach Tybee Island nearly thrity minutes later. The traffic was just too hectic.

By the time Press returned to the beach, the guy still hadn't arrived. Even more pissed off, Press made a u-turn, heading towards his truck. The beach itself wasn't crowded so spotting the pink would've stood out like a sore thumb.

"Excuse me sir. You mind coming with me," some random security guard motioned, interrupting the pity party that press was throwing.

"For what?"

"A burglary just took place around this area and you fit the description of the suspect. Just need to ask you some questions. You mind?"

"Actually, I do."

"I wasn't asking," the guard returned, reaching for Press's arm. Back up was called to assist with this matter. After a brief struggle, the guards finally managed to overthrow Press's strength. Afterwards he was took to a isolated building that sat to the rear of the beach.

"What the fuck's your name pal? Earl?" Press asked, reading the security guards name tag. At this point they just entered the building.

"Earl, I hope you know you fucked up tombout Imma thief n shit. My pops the Chief of police. Surprised? Are you a fan? Because I can get you a autograph. He'll sign your death certificate. *Translation*: you'll be terminated."

"See what you need to do is fall the fuck back, ol' fake ass police. You don't even have a gun. What you gon'do, hit somebody with dat night stick? I was the police for real mothafucka."

"Take off your clothes and put this on," the security guard demanded.

"Make me. Rental cop. Take me to jail."

The security guard searched Press and pulled out the letter that was handed to him by the kid. He read it briefly and tried to make Press put on some swimming trucks. But Press was uncooperative.

After refusing for a second time, the security guard pulled out his walkey talkey and initated a conversation between him and an unknown source. This event made Press even angrier.

"Looks like it's about to rain."

"You fake—wait, what?" Press asked unbelievably mid-sentence.

"I said. Looks like it's about to rain," the security guard repeated, Leaving Press speechless, and in a complete state of shock.

◆ ◆ ◆

"Hi. How are you Mr. Mcgurt? You don't mind if I call you Mr. Mcgurt, do you? Or would you prefer Preston?"

"Press is cool."

"Ok, Press. Everyone calls me Flores. Nice to finally meet you," the Columbian drug overlord smiled extending his right hand and introducing himself.

Press shook Flores's hand and proceeded to walk along the beach with him. After changing into the swimming trunks, the security guard directed press to the beach where he was met by the spanish kingpin, Flores, and his entourage. Neither member of Flores's gang had on pink. The mere suggestion was to throw press off (just in case he tried to set them up) by creating a diversion. The swimming trunks was to ensure that he wasn't wearing a wire.

"So the Chief of Police's your father? I'm impressed," Flores complimented.

"How so?"

"I'm a honest guy press. And no offense. But I don't see the resemblance."

"None taken."

"You know Press. I have to admit. I arranged this meeting extremely apprehensively. I just feel like you and I aren't compatible. In fact, the only reason why I'm here is because of three little words, Noble Drew Ali. He's a dear friend of mine. So as a favor to him, I agreed. But that's the only reason I allowed you to speak with me. Understand?"

"I understand."

"Good. Now. What is it that you wanted to discuss? Noble Drew said you needed work. What other skills do you have besides law enforcement? I just opened a construction company in the historic downtown district. I may have some openings," Flores informed, as they walked slowly on the beach.

"With all due respect Mr. Flores. I think you know I didn't come here to talk about that kind of work."

"Well what type of work are you interested in pursuing?"

Press held his breath in before he spoke again. He chose his words very carefully.

"I need fifty keys."

"I see. Because I'm Columbian you automatically assume I'm a dealer?"

"I meant no harm."

"So you say. My businesses are all legitimate. I'm not involved in anything illegal. Sorry to disappoint you my friend."

"Look Flores. I know you're skeptical because of my past profession. But who could be a better dope boy than an ex cop? Exactly. No-one. I know the law like the back of my hand. I was a police officer for five years Flores, five long fuckin years. I still have friends on the force that can be ours eyes and ears," Press convinced.

"Plus, I have a lot of family members to help me get rid of the shit. And I've interacted with people from all walks of life, so my clientele's gon' come from more than one ethnic group. Which means we don't have to win a spelling bee to see capitol."

"And judging by the way you dress, I can tell you like capitol, and I'm not talking Washington DC. So if that's racial profiling, then fine, I guess I'm guilty. You'll have to excuse me Flores. But I'm an honest guy as well. My mouth's irrevocably unfiltered."

"When I take an oath, I honor that oath, and it's death before dishonor. I'm a man of my word Flores. Noble Drew wouldn't've vouched for me otherwise."

Flores was thinking long and hard about press's comments.

"With my knowledge of the law and political ties we can take over this city. I can help you make more money than you can imagine. And although you don't think that me and the Chief favor, he is my dad, and you need his resources, which aren't for sale. Unless of course, you go through me, his blood relative, and only son."

Flores and his entourage just continued to walk on the beach. After giving Press's proposal some more thought, he stopped walking.

"Sorry press. I just can't help you. Fifty kilos? Not possible."

Disappointed, Press stormed off. He wasn't going to kiss no-one's ass. He'd just have to find another plug he reasoned, which was easier said than done. Maybe he was in over his head? Maybe he just needed to take his ass home and get ready for work tomorrow he pouted.

"How about ten?" Flores said gently before Press made it to far out of his sight.

Press looked back at Flores and returned his gaze. All he could do was smile on the inside as he headed back towards the group.

No, It didn't look like it was about to rain.

But Press was definitely about to make it snow.

CHAPTER 26

Family ties

The next day Press was up bright and early. This happened frequently whenever he felt anxiety. He picked up the phone and dialed his convict cousin, Adam.

"Speak."

"Yo. Sup?"

"Shit. Who dis?"

"Your cuzin Negro. Press."

"Oh. Wad up cuz?"

"Chillin. On a mission. I need to talk to you face to face."

"About what?"

"I'll tell you later. Wyd?"

"Getting ready for work."

"Oh yea, I almost forgot. Grocery boy."

"You gotta lot of nerve calling me this early wit jokes. That's why your ex getting smashed by a partner of mines."

"Good for her."

"Adam, you need a nickname. Ace, it's what I'm calling you from now on. I need you to meet me at auntie's later to talk business. Be there. On time."

After ending the call with Ace, Press pulled up on Broughton Street and parked his truck. He had a lot on his agenda today. Good thing he got there early before the place was packed. It was always that way when you decided to pay your utility bill late. Later, he'd probably stop by to check on his mom. At least until six a clock. During that time, press had a real essential meeting that he had to attend. The night before, he called Tandra and Eve, insisting that they all meet. Eve and Tandra made plans a head of time allegedy. But the resistance was removed from the conversation once the term money was used. Ace on the other hand was game from the start.

Press and Ace's friendship blossomed after Charlotte became Ace's probation officer. After all the time that passed she was still his PO. Ace, who was finally doing right for once, was the only remaining link between the two.

Earlier, Ace mentioned that charlotte was dating one of his friends. As much as press hated to admit it, this information was alarming. He hadn't spoken to charlotte in months so why was he bothered that she chose to move on?

Press walked inside of the building and stood in line. Immediately he felt like every single eye ball was protruding his way, two in particular. They belonged to this extremely gorgeous petite young stallion that looked familiar.

"Don't I know you from somewhere?" Press directed this question to the above-mentioned young lady that stood in line next to him. She had on a coogi dress, designer shoes (that he wasn't familiar with), and an angel face. The kind that every man dreams about and wants to wake up next to. She wasn't a K. Michelle in the darier category, but her ass was above the standard size, and she was blessed in the facial department.

"No—I don't think so," Halle Barry's protégée said.

Embarrassed, Press turned around and continued to wait in line. He was really trying to spark a conversation with her on the slide. But the way she brushed him off so easily was offensive.

You aint all dat anyway bitch. Fuck you too then. Go give that hoarse back his hair, Mr. Ed. Bald-head ass.

After cursing her out under his breath, and paying his utility bill, Press headed back outside towards his truck. He had a lot on his agenda today and time was of an essence.

"Hey. Mr. You dropped this," Halle Barry's protégée discovered, running out of the utility place behind him. She handed him his receipt.

"Thanks."

"No problem."

"Say. Are you sure I don't know you? Because you look familiar?"

"No. You don't know me. But we have crossed paths."

"I knew it," press blushed.

Sensing his uncertainty, Halle's protégée smiled. "You really don't remember me?"

"Not really."

"Remember. That cop, who I'm assuming was your friend, tried to holla at my friend. We were at the doughnut shop."

"That's rite. She must've turned him down a million times. But he just wouldn't quit. You still remember dat? That was years ago."

"Remember dat? How can I forget? That day, I reconciled with society."

"You were in pris---Hol on---Ms. Blink is your PO? That's where I know you from. The probation office.

"I see someone's recovered from altimers."

"There's no cure for altimers."

"You know what I mean. Smart ass. The good news is that I completed my probation. Thank god."

"I'm Aundrea by the way," Halle Barry's protégée extended her hand for press to shake. She was being overly friendly.

They conversated a little while longer. Aundrea was currently attending Savannah State University, pursuing a degree in race relations. She lived on Savannah's southside. These were just a few details that Aundrea briefly shared with Press about herself.

After exchanging numbers, they departed ways, each of them heading in the opposite direction. Once inside the truck, Press smiled broadly to himself. He didn't know much about the girl but he intended to change that. In Press's mind, aundrea was the type of girl that a man sports on his arm to make others jealous. Maybe she was wifey material. Maybe not.

Who's Charlotte? Press thought dismissively. Because after meeting Aundrea, he just couldn't remember.

◆ ◆ ◆

When six a clock arrived Press pulled up to his aunt Tandra's house. After a brief knock, Tandra answered, greeting the lastest edition to the meeting. He entered the living room with swift speed failing to greet the meeting's attendees.

"You can't speak? Big ass head," Eve teased, as Press flew pass her. The three of them had all gathered just like he asked.

"Aunte. You got something in here cold to drink? And I don't mean cheap beer."

"Excuse you. When did you become a baller? Freeway Rick lost."

"There's some hennie in the fridge. Help yourself."

After retrieving the alchol, Press came back to the living room and remained standing. Everyone else was seated.

"Now. As you probably heard shit has changed dramatically these last few months. I lost my girl, two jobs, and almost my freedom. I know yall still think of me as the police. But my law-abiding days are over. Today, Imma entrepreneur. And I want yall to be apart of my organization."

After hearing Press's words, they exchanged funny looks amongst one another.

Noticing this, he continued to give his spiel. "Today's a new day people. I took an oath to uphold the law thinking that I'd make a difference in the community. But eventually, I found out that there's just as much criminals on the force as they are in the streets, if not more. These local police officers are gang members, believe it or not. They just don't wear red and blue flags, they wear badges. Their operations go undetected because they're provided with the latest technology, compliments of our deceptive, ignorant, and stupid ass government."

"Starting here, rite now, Today, I'm making my own rules. Which brings me to my next point. Rule #1. Ten percent of our profits go back to the community. We pay our taxes every quarter in laymen terms. Rule#2. Under no circumstances do we do business with anyone unless we have a working knowledge about their personal life. The more we know, the greater our chances are of surviving an indictment. I don't care if it pertains to their family, extended family, friends, etc, all information's good information, don't disregard anything. Without a snitch, the judicial system is fucking lost, trust me on this yall. If a mufucka wants to be master splinter, we need to be shredder, if you get my drift," Press preached, speaking the gospel like a pastor at a Sunday church service.

Confused, they exchanged looks amongst each other again but this time in a more comedic fashion. What in the hell was Press suggesting? They wondered because to them this wasn't making any sense.

Observing the confusion, he continued. "Now. I have ten kilos of pure Colombian cocaine. I'll keep four, and yall can split the rest. Everything else we'll figure out along the way."

Finally realizing what Press was proposing, they all bursted out with laughter. They never suspected in a million lifetimes that press would call this meeting to form a criminal enterprise. For years Press was viewed as an outcast. Their flesh & blood, but a lame, never the less. The trio loved him regardless of his profession. But they never dreamed in a million years that he'd be anything besides a cop. In fact, they were shocked to hear that he decided to take a job at Bank of America let alone a BP gas station.

Press's transition would be the center of future jokes. The Mcgurt family was known to clown. And press was the biggest circus of them all. The Chief of police's son, Robocop, had chosen a life of crime, which was beyond his standard characteristic traits and extremely hilarious.

For years, press provided protection to the city of savannah's citizen's.

Now, it was time to serve them.

www.ingramcontent.com/pod-product-compliance
Lightning Source LLC
Chambersburg PA
CBHW020912180626
46816CB00007BA/2359